DETECTIVE
STORIES

KINGFISHER
Larousse Kingfisher Chambers Inc.
95 Madison Avenue
New York, New York 10016

First published in 1998
(HC) 2 4 6 8 10 9 7 5 3 1
(PB) 2 4 6 8 10 9 7 5 3 1

LIBRARY OF CONGRESS CATALOGING-IN-PUBLICATION DATA
Detective stories / [chosen by Philip Pullman] . illustrated by Nick
Hardcastle. —1st ed.
p. cm. — (Story Library)
Contents: The speckled band / Arthur Conan Doyle—The
inspiration of M. Budd / Dorothy L. Sayers—Emil and the
detectives / Erich Kastner—Butch minds the baby / Damon Runyon—
Murder at St. Oswald's / Michael Underwood—The cross of Lorraine
/ Isaac Asimov—The adventure of the Egyptian tomb. / Agatha
Christie—Cold money / Ellery Queen—Fingerprinting a ghost /
Tony Fletcher—It's a hard world / Andrew Vachss—Maddened by
mystery, or, The defective detective / Stephen Leacock.
1. Detective and mystery stories. 2. Children's stories.
[1 Mystery and detective stories. 2. Short stories.] I. Pullman,
Philip, 1946- . II. Hardcastle, Nick, ill. III. Series.
PZ5.D48 1998
[Fic]—dc21 97-41357 CIP AC

ISBN 0-7534-5157-3 (HC)
ISBN 0-7534-5146-8 (PB)

Printed and bound in Great Britain by
Caledonian International Book Manufacturing Ltd., Glasgow

DETECTIVE
STORIES

CHOSEN BY
PHILIP PULLMAN

ILLUSTRATED BY
NICK HARDCASTLE

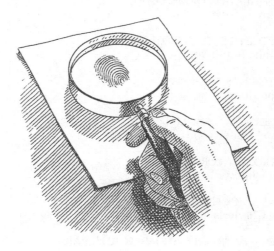

KINGFISHER
NEW YORK

CONTENTS

INTRODUCTION

O F ALL THE HEROES in story, one of my favorites is the detective. The lone figure in the trench coat going down dark streets in search of a mysterious killer—the hawk-eyed man with pipe and deerstalker hat peering at a minute clue through a magnifying glass—the young woman venturing into desperate danger from which only her intelligence and courage can save her—once they begin to track the criminal down, we can't help but follow. The first story I read that chilled me to the very marrow and made me tremble with fear and excitement was a story about the greatest detective of all, Sherlock Holmes, and it's in this collection.

Detective stories have a long history. There is one in the Bible, in which the young prophet Daniel proves the guilt of two old men by showing that their stories differ in one important detail. And they are also as up to date as today's news. The latest generation of detectives, whether in books or on the TV screen, is as popular as ever.

If detective fiction had a golden age, it was roughly during the sixty years or so after the first Sherlock Holmes story appeared, in 1887. Many of the patterns that were set then have never been changed. The detective is a striking and occasionally eccentric figure, whose adventures are often narrated by a friend—someone less odd than the central figure, less gifted, but more normal, more like us. Even when the detective is a member of a large police force, and not a private investigator, he or she is very often a bit of a maverick. We readers like to feel that our heroes and heroines have to fight the system as well as simply catch the villain. It makes their triumph more satisfying, and it reflects the way we often feel ourselves as we struggle with the pointless rules and petty restrictions of school or work.

The sort of detective stories I enjoy most are the ones that give us a sense of the world around the detective. A puzzle in a vacuum is only a puzzle (though some of those can be fun too, like the ones by Raymond Smullyan you'll find in the book); but to be a satisfying story, the mystery must also evoke a world we can enjoy spending a little time in. The crooks and gamblers of Damon Runyan's Broadway live in such a world, and so does the dapper little figure of Hercule Poirot, among the wealthy amateur archaeologists and the sinister shadowy figures of Egyptian gods. And the most vivid world of all is the gaslit, foggy London which for so many readers is the classic setting of the English murder story.

So in this collection you'll find stories that take you to many different worlds. There are crimes ranging from cold-blooded murder to the kidnapping of a dog—detectives both famous and obscure, old and young—settings that include an ancient Egyptian tomb, a sinister English country house, the streets of New York.

And for good measure there are one or two funny stories as well.

As Sherlock Holmes said to Dr. Watson: "The game is afoot!"

Philip Pullman
November 1997

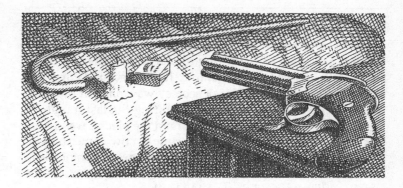

THE SPECKLED BAND

ARTHUR CONAN DOYLE

No collection of detective stories would be complete without Sherlock Holmes. Everyone can recognize him, even in outline: the pipe, the deerstalker hat, the keen sharp-featured profile are famous the world over, and have been for over a hundred years.

Most of the stories are narrated by Holmes's great friend, Dr. Watson, and this is one of the very best. It begins in their comfortable rooms in Baker Street, and culminates in a night of extraordinary suspense and horror as Holmes and Watson wait in the darkened murder room for the appearance of the speckled band, which has caused the horrifying death of a young woman.

But what can it be?

IN GLANCING OVER my notes of the seventy odd cases in which I have during the last eight years studied the methods of my friend Sherlock Holmes, I find many tragic, some comic, a large number merely strange, but none commonplace; for, working as he did rather for the love of his art than for the acquirement of wealth, he refused to associate himself with any investigation which did not tend toward the unusual, and even the fantastic. Of all these varied cases, however, I cannot recall any which presented more singular features than that which was associated with the well-known

Surrey family of the Roylotts of Stoke Moran. The events in question occurred in the early days of my association with Holmes, when we were sharing rooms as bachelors, in Baker Street. It is possible that I might have placed them upon record before, but a promise of secrecy was made at the time, from which I have only been freed during the last month by the untimely death of the lady to whom the pledge was given. It is perhaps as well that the facts should now come to light, for I have reasons to know there are widespread rumors as to the death of Dr. Grimesby Roylott which tend to make the matter even more terrible than the truth.

It was early in April, in the year '83, that I woke one morning to find Sherlock Holmes standing, fully dressed, by the side of my bed. He was a late riser as a rule, and, as the clock on the mantelpiece showed me that it was only a quarter past seven, I blinked up at him in some surprise, and perhaps just a little resentment, for I was myself regular in my habits.

"Very sorry to knock you up, Watson," said he, "but it's the common lot this morning. Mrs. Hudson has been knocked up, she retorted upon me, and I on you."

"What is it, then? A fire?"

"No, a client. It seems that a young lady has arrived in a considerable state of excitement, who insists upon seeing me. She is waiting now in the sitting room. Now, when young ladies wander about the metropolis at this hour of the morning, and knock sleepy people up out of their beds, I presume that it is something very pressing which they have to communicate. Should it prove to be an interesting case, you would, I am sure, wish to follow it from the outset. I thought at any rate that I should call you, and give you the chance."

"My dear fellow, I would not miss it for anything."

I had no keener pleasure than in following Holmes in his professional investigations, and in admiring the rapid deductions, as swift as intuitions, and yet always founded on a logical basis, with which he unraveled the problems which were submitted to him. I rapidly threw on my clothes, and was ready in a few minutes to accompany my friend down to the sitting room. A lady dressed in black and heavily veiled, who had been sitting in the window, rose as we entered.

"Good morning, madam," said Holmes cheerily. "My name is Sherlock Holmes. This is my intimate friend and associate, Dr. Watson, before whom you can speak as freely as before myself. Ha, I am glad to see that Mrs. Hudson has had the good sense to light the fire. Pray draw up to it, and I shall order you a cup of hot coffee, for I observe that you are shivering."

"It is not cold which makes me shiver," said the woman in a low voice, changing her seat as requested.

"What then?"

"It is fear, Mr. Holmes. It is terror." She raised her veil as she spoke, and we could see that she was indeed in a pitiable state of agitation, her face all drawn and gray, with restless, frightened eyes, like those of some hunted animal. Her features and figure were those of a woman of thirty, but her hair was shot with premature gray, and her expression was weary and haggard. Sherlock Holmes ran her over with one of his quick, all-comprehensive glances.

"You must not fear," said he soothingly, bending forward and patting her forearm. "We shall soon set matters right, I have no doubt. You have come in by train this morning, I see."

"You know me, then?"

"No, but I observe the second half of a return ticket in the palm of your left glove. You must have started early and yet you had a good drive in a dog-cart, along heavy roads, before you reached the station."

The lady gave a violent start, and stared in bewilderment at my companion.

"There is no mystery, my dear madam," said he, smiling. "The left arm of your jacket is spattered with mud in no less than seven places. The marks are perfectly fresh. There is no vehicle save a dog-cart which throws up mud in that way, and then only when you sit on the left-hand side of the driver."

"Whatever your reasons may be, you are perfectly correct," said she. "I started from home before six, reached

Leatherhead at twenty past, and came in by the first train to Waterloo. Sir, I can stand this strain no longer, I shall go mad if it continues. I have no one to turn to—none, save only one, who cares for me, and he, poor fellow, can be of little aid. I have heard of you, Mr. Holmes; I have heard of you from Mrs. Farintosh, whom you helped in the hour of her sore need. It was from her that I had your address. Oh, sir, do you not think you could help me too, and at least throw a little light through the dense darkness which surrounds me? At present it is out of my power to reward you for your services, but in a month or two I shall be married, with the control of my own income, and then at least you shall not find me ungrateful."

Holmes turned to his desk, and unlocking it, drew out a small casebook which he consulted.

"Farintosh," said he. "Ah, yes, I recall the case; it was concerned with an opal tiara. I think it was before your time, Watson. I can only say, madam, that I shall be happy to devote the same care to your case as I did to that of your friend. As to reward, my profession is its reward; but you are at liberty to defray whatever expenses I may be put to, at the time which suits you best. And now I beg that you will lay before us everything that may help us in forming an opinion on the matter."

"Alas!" replied our visitor. "The very horror of my situation lies in the fact that my fears are so vague, and my suspicions depend so entirely upon small points, which might seem trivial to another, that even he to whom of all others I have a right to look for help and advice looks upon all that I tell him about it as the fancies of a nervous woman. He does not say so, but I can read it from his soothing answers and averted eyes. But I have heard, Mr. Holmes, that you can see deeply into the manifold wickedness of the human heart. You may advise me how to walk amid the dangers which encompass me."

"I am all attention, madam."

"My name is Helen Stoner, and I am living with my stepfather, who is the last survivor of one of the oldest Saxon families in England, the Roylotts of Stoke Moran, on the Western border of Surrey."

Holmes nodded his head. "The name is familiar to me," said he.

"The family was at one time among the richest in England, and the estate extended over the borders into Berkshire in the north, and Hampshire in the west. In the last century, however, four successive heirs were of a dissolute and wasteful disposition, and the family ruin was eventually completed by a gambler, in the days of the Regency. Nothing was left save a few acres of ground and the two-hundred-year-old house, which is itself crushed under a heavy mortgage. The last squire dragged out his existence there, living the horrible life of an aristocratic pauper; but his only son, my stepfather, seeing that he must adapt himself to the new conditions, obtained an advance from a relative, which enabled him to take a medical degree, and went out to Calcutta, where, by his professional skill and his force of character, he established a large practice. In a fit of anger, however, caused by some robberies which had been perpetrated in the house, he beat his native butler to death, and narrowly escaped a capital sentence. As it was, he suffered a long term of imprisonment, and afterwards returned to England a morose and disappointed man.

"When Dr. Roylott was in India he married my mother, Mrs. Stoner, the young widow of Major-General Stoner, of the Bengal Artillery. My sister Julia and I were twins, and we were only two years old at the time of my mother's remarriage. She had a considerable sum of money, not less than a thousand a year, and this she bequeathed to Dr. Roylott entirely whilst we resided with him, with a provision that a certain annual sum should be allowed to each of us in the event of our marriage. Shortly after our return to England my mother died—she was killed eight years ago in a railway accident near Crewe. Dr. Roylott then abandoned his attempts to establish himself in practice in London, and took us to live with him in the ancestral house at Stoke Moran. The money which my mother had left was enough for all our wants, and there seemed no obstacle to our happiness.

"But a terrible change came over our stepfather about this time. Instead of making friends and exchanging visits with our neighbors, who had at first been overjoyed to see a Roylott of Stoke Moran back in the old family seat, he shut himself up in his house, and seldom came out save to indulge in ferocious quarrels with whoever might cross his path. Violence of temper approaching to mania has been hereditary in the men of the family, and in my stepfather's case it had, I believe, been intensified by his long residence in the tropics. A series of disgraceful brawls took place, two of which ended in the police-court, until at last he became the terror of the village, and the folks would fly at his approach, for he is a man of immense strength, and absolutely uncontrollable in his anger.

"Last week he hurled the local blacksmith over a parapet into a stream and it was only by paying over all the money that I could gather together that I was able to avert another public exposure. He had no friends at all save the wandering gypsies, and he would give these vagabonds leave to encamp upon the few acres of bramble-covered land which represent the family estate, and would accept in return the hospitality of their tents, wandering away with them sometimes for weeks on end. He has a passion also for Indian animals, which are sent over to him by a correspondent, and he has at this moment a cheetah and a baboon, which wander freely over his grounds, and are feared by the villagers almost as much as their master.

"You can imagine from what I say that my poor sister Julia and I had no great pleasure in our lives. No servant would stay with us, and for a long time we did all the work of the house. She was but thirty at the time of her death, and yet her hair had already begun to whiten, even as mine has."

"Your sister is dead, then?"

"She died just two years ago, and it is of her death that I wish to speak to you. You can understand that, living the life which I have described, we were little likely to see anyone of our own age and position. We had, however, an aunt, my mother's maiden sister, Miss Honoria Westphail, who lives near Harrow, and we were occasionally allowed to pay short visits at this lady's house. Julia went there at Christmas two years ago, and met there a half-pay Major of Marines, to whom she became engaged. My stepfather learned of the engagement when my sister returned, and offered no objection to the marriage; but within a fortnight of the day which had been fixed for the wedding, the terrible event occurred which has deprived me of my only companion."

Sherlock Holmes had been leaning back in his chair with his eyes closed, and his head sunk in a cushion, but he half opened his lids now, and glanced across at his visitor.

"Pray be precise as to details," said he.

"It is easy for me to be so, for every event of that dreadful time is seared into my memory. The manor house is, as I have already said, very old, and only one wing is now inhabited. The bedrooms in this wing are on the ground floor, the sitting rooms being in the central block of the buildings. Of these bedrooms the first is Dr. Roylott's, the second my sister's, and the third my own. There is no communication between them, but they all open out into the same corridor. Do I make myself plain?"

"Perfectly so."

"The windows of the three rooms open out upon the lawn. That fatal night Dr. Roylott had gone to his room early, though we knew that he had not retired to rest, for my sister was troubled by the smell of the strong Indian cigars which it was his custom to smoke. She left her room, therefore, and came into mine, where she sat for some time, chatting about her approaching wedding. At eleven o'clock she rose to leave me, but she paused at the door and looked back.

" 'Tell me, Helen,' said she, 'have you ever heard anyone whistle in the dead of the night?'

" 'Never,' said I.

" 'I suppose that you could not possibly whistle yourself in your sleep?'

" 'Certainly not. But why?'

" 'Because during the last few nights I have always, about three in the morning, heard a low clear whistle. I am a light sleeper, and it has awakened me. I cannot tell where it came from—perhaps from the next room, perhaps from the lawn. I thought that I would just ask you whether you had heard it.'

" 'No, I have not. It must be those wretched gypsies in the plantation.'

" 'Very likely. And yet if it were on the lawn I wonder that you did not hear it also.'

" 'Ah, but I sleep more heavily than you.'

" 'Well, it is of no great consequence, at any rate,' she smiled back at me, closed my door, and a few moments later I heard her key turn in the lock."

"Indeed," said Holmes. "Was it your custom always to lock yourselves in at night?"

"Always."

"And why?"

"I think that I mentioned to you that the Doctor kept a cheetah and a baboon. We had no feeling of security unless our doors were locked."

"Quite so. Pray proceed with your statement."

"I could not sleep that night. A vague feeling of impending misfortune impressed me. My sister and I, you will recollect, were twins, and you know how subtle are the links which bind two souls which are so closely allied. It was a wild night. The wind was howling outside, and the rain was beating and splashing against the windows. Suddenly, amidst all the hubbub of the gale, there burst forth the wild scream of a terrified woman. I knew that it was my sister's voice. I sprang from my bed, wrapped a shawl round me, and rushed into the corridor. As I opened my door I seemed to hear a low whistle, such as my sister described, and a few moments later a clanging sound, as if a mass of metal had fallen. As I ran down the passage my sister's door was unlocked, and revolved slowly upon its hinges. I stared at it horror-stricken, not knowing what was about to issue from it. By the light of the corridor lamp I saw my sister appear at the opening, her face blanched with terror, her hands groping for help, her whole figure swaying to and fro like that of a drunkard. I ran to her and threw my arms round her, but at that moment her knees seemed to give way and she fell to the ground. She writhed as one who is in terrible pain, and her limbs were dreadfully convulsed. At first I thought that she had not recognized me, but as I bent over her she suddenly shrieked out in a voice which I shall never forget, 'Oh, my God! Helen! It was the band! The speckled band!' There was something else which she would fain have said, and she stabbed with her finger into the air in the direction of the Doctor's room, but a fresh convulsion seized her and choked her words. I rushed out, calling loudly for my stepfather, and I met him hastening from his room in his dressing-gown. When he reached my sister's side she was unconscious, and though he poured brandy down her throat, and sent for medical aid from the village, all efforts were in vain, for she slowly sank and died without having recovered her consciousness. Such was the dreadful end of my beloved sister."

"One moment," said Holmes: "are you sure about this whistle and metallic sound? Could you swear to it?"

"That was what the county coroner asked me at the inquiry. It is my strong impression that I heard it, and yet among the crash of the gale, and the creaking of an old house, I may possibly have been deceived."

"Was your sister dressed?"

"No, she was in her nightdress. In her right hand was found the charred stump of a match, and in her left a matchbox."

"Showing that she had struck a light and looked about her when the alarm took place. That is important. And what conclusions did the coroner come to?"

"He investigated the case with great care, for Dr. Roylott's conduct had long been notorious in the county, but he was unable to find any satisfactory cause of death. My evidence showed that the door had been fastened upon the inner side, and the windows were blocked by old-fashioned shutters with broad iron bars, which were secured every night. The walls were carefully sounded, and were shown to be quite solid all round, and the flooring was also thoroughly examined, with the same result. The chimney is wide, but is barred up by four large staples. It is certain, therefore, that my sister was quite alone when she met her end. Besides, there were no marks of any violence upon her."

"How about poison?"

"The doctors examined her for it, but without success."

"What do you think that this unfortunate lady died of, then?"

"It is my belief that she died of pure fear and nervous shock, though what it was which frightened her I cannot imagine."

"Were there gypsies in the plantation at the time?"

"Yes, there are nearly always some there."

"Ah, and what did you gather from this allusion to a band—a speckled band?"

"Sometimes I have thought that it was merely the wild talk of delirium, sometimes that it may have referred to some band of people, perhaps to these very gypsies in the plantation. I do not know whether the spotted handkerchiefs which so many of them wear over their heads might have suggested the strange adjective which she used."

Holmes shook his head like a man who is far from being satisfied.

"These are very deep waters," said he; "pray go on with your narrative."

"Two years have passed since then, and my life has been until lately lonelier than ever. A month ago, however, a dear friend, whom I have known for many years, has done me the honor to ask my hand in marriage. His name is Armitage—Percy Armitage—the second son of Mr. Armitage, of Crane Water, near Reading. My stepfather has offered no opposition to the match, and we are to be married in the course of the spring. Two days ago some repairs were started in the west wing of the building, and my bedroom wall has been pierced, so that I have had to move into the chamber in which my sister died, and to sleep in the very bed in which she slept. Imagine, then, my thrill of terror when last night, as I lay awake, thinking over her terrible fate, I suddenly heard in the silence of the night the low whistle which had been the herald of her own death. I sprang up and lit the lamp, but nothing was to be seen in the room. I was too shaken to go to bed again, however, so I dressed, and as soon as it was daylight I slipped down, got a dog-cart at the Crown Inn, which is opposite, and drove to Leatherhead, from whence I have come on this morning, with the one object of seeing you and asking your advice."

"You have done wisely," said my friend. "But have you told me all?"

"Yes, all."

"Miss Stoner, you have not. You are screening your stepfather."

"Why, what do you mean?"

For answer Holmes pushed back the frill of black lace which fringed the hand that lay upon our visitor's knee. Five little livid spots, the marks of four fingers and a thumb, were printed upon the white wrist.

"You have been cruelly used," said Holmes.

The lady colored deeply, and covered over her injured wrist. "He is a hard man," she said, "and perhaps he hardly knows his own strength."

There was a long silence, during which Holmes leaned his chin upon his hands and stared into the crackling fire.

"This is a very deep business," he said at last. "There are a thousand details which I should desire to know before I decide upon our course of action. Yet we have not a moment to lose. If we were to come to Stoke Moran today, would it be possible for us to see over these rooms without the knowledge of your stepfather?"

"As it happens, he spoke of coming into town today upon some most important business. It is probable that he will be away all day, and that there would be nothing to disturb you.

We have a housekeeper now, but she is old and foolish, and I could easily get her out of the way."

"Excellent. You are not averse to this trip, Watson?"

"By no means."

"Then we shall both come. What are you going to do yourself?"

"I have one or two things which I would wish to do now that I am in town. But I shall return by the twelve o'clock train, so as to be there in time for your coming."

"And you may expect us early in the afternoon. I have myself some small business matters to attend to. Will you not wait and breakfast?"

"No, I must go. My heart is lightened already since I have confided my trouble to you. I shall look forward to seeing you again this afternoon." She dropped her thick black veil over her face, and glided from the room.

"And what do you think of it all, Watson?" asked Sherlock Holmes, leaning back in his chair.

"It seems to me to be a most dark and sinister business."

"Dark enough and sinister enough."

"Yet if the lady is correct in saying that the flooring and walls are sound, and that the door, window, and chimney are impassable, then her sister must have been undoubtedly alone when she met her mysterious end."

"What becomes, then, of these nocturnal whistles, and what of the very peculiar words of the dying woman?"

"I cannot think."

"When you combine the ideas of whistles at night, the presence of a band of gypsies who are on intimate terms with this old doctor, the fact that we have every reason to believe that the doctor has an interest in preventing his stepdaughter's marriage, the dying allusion to a band, and finally, the fact that Miss Helen Stoner heard a metallic clang, which might have been caused by one of those metal bars which secured the shutters falling back into their place, I think there is good ground to think that the mystery may be cleared along those lines."

"But what, then, did the gypsies do?"

"I cannot imagine."

"I see many objections to any such a theory."

"And so do I. It is precisely for that reason that we are going to Stoke Moran this day. I want to see whether the objections are fatal, or if they may be explained away. But what, in the name of the devil!"

The ejaculation had been drawn from my companion by the fact that our door had been suddenly dashed open, and that a huge man framed himself in the aperture. His costume was a peculiar mixture of the professional and of the agricultural, having a black top hat, a long frock-coat, and a pair of high gaiters, with a hunting crop swinging in his hand. So tall was he that his hat actually brushed the crossbar of the doorway, and his breadth seemed to span it across from side to side. A large face, seared with a thousand wrinkles, burned yellow with the sun, and marked with every evil passion, was turned from one to the other of us, while his deep-set, bile-shot eyes, and the high thin fleshless nose, gave him somewhat the resemblance to a fierce old bird of prey.

"Which of you is Holmes?" asked this apparition.

"My name, sir, but you have the advantage of me," said my companion quietly.

"I am Dr. Grimesby Roylott, of Stoke Moran."

"Indeed, Doctor," said Holmes blandly. "Pray take a seat."

"I will do nothing of the kind. My stepdaughter has been here. I have traced her. What has she been saying to you?"

"It is a little cold for the time of the year," said Holmes.

"What has she been saying to you?" screamed the old man furiously.

"But I have heard that the crocuses promise well," continued my companion imperturbably.

"Ha! You put me off, do you?" said our new visitor, taking a step forward, and shaking his hunting crop. "I know you, you scoundrel! I have heard of you before. You are Holmes the meddler."

My friend smiled.

"Holmes the busybody!"

His smile broadened.

"Holmes the Scotland Yard jack-in-office."

Holmes chuckled heartily. "Your conversation is most entertaining," said he. "When you go out close the door, for there is a decided draft."

"I will go when I have had my say. Don't you dare to meddle with my affairs. I know that Miss Stoner has been here —I traced her! I am a dangerous man to fall foul of! See here." He stepped swiftly forward, seized the poker, and bent it into a curve with his huge brown hands.

"See that you keep yourself out of my grip," he snarled, and hurling the twisted poker into the fireplace, he strode out of the room.

"He seems a very amiable person," said Holmes, laughing. "I am not quite so bulky, but if he had remained I might have shown him that my grip was not much more feeble than his own." As he spoke he picked up the steel poker, and with a sudden effort straightened it out again.

"Fancy his having the insolence to confound me with the official detective force! This incident gives zest to our investigation, however, and I only trust that our little friend will not suffer from her imprudence in allowing this brute to trace her. And now, Watson, we shall order breakfast, and afterwards I shall walk down to Doctors' Commons, where I hope to get some data which may help us in this matter."

It was nearly one o'clock when Sherlock Holmes returned from his excursion. He held in his hand a sheet of blue paper, scrawled over with notes and figures.

"I have seen the will of the deceased wife," said he. "To determine its exact meaning I have been obliged to work out the present prices of the investments with which it is concerned. The total income, which at the time of the wife's death was little short of £1,100, is now through the fall in agricultural prices not more than £750. Each daughter can claim an income of £250, in case of marriage. It is evident, therefore, that if both girls had married, this beauty would have had a mere pittance, while even one of them would cripple him to a serious extent. My morning's work has not been wasted, since it has proved that he has the very strongest motives for standing in the way of anything of the sort. And now, Watson, this is too serious for dawdling, especially as the old man is aware that we are interesting ourselves in his affairs, so if you are ready we shall call a cab and drive to Waterloo. I should be very much obliged if you would slip your revolver into your pocket. An Eley's No. 2 is an excellent argument with gentlemen who can twist steel pokers into knots. That and a toothbrush are, I think, all that we need."

At Waterloo we were fortunate in catching a train for Leatherhead, where we hired a trap at the station inn, and drove for four or five miles through the lovely Surrey lanes. It was a perfect day, with a bright sun and a few fleecy clouds in the heavens. The trees and wayside hedges were just throwing out their first green shoots, and the air was full of the pleasant smell of the moist earth. To me at least there was a strange contrast between the sweet promise of the spring and this sinister quest upon which we were engaged. My companion sat in front of the trap, his arms folded, his hat pulled down over his eyes, and his chin sunk upon his breast, buried in the deepest thought. Suddenly, however, he started, tapped me on the shoulder, and pointed over the meadows.

"Look there!" said he.

A heavily timbered park stretched up in a gentle slope, thickening into a grove at the highest point. From amidst the branches there jutted out the gray gables and high rooftree of a very old mansion.

"Stoke Moran?" said he.

"Yes, sir, that be the house of Dr. Grimesby Roylott," remarked the driver.

"There is some building going on there," said Holmes: "that is where we are going."

"There's the village," said the driver, pointing to a cluster of roofs some distance to the left; "but if you want to get to the house, you'll find it shorter to go over this stile, and so by the footpath over the fields. There it is, where the lady is walking."

"And the lady, I fancy, is Miss Stoner," observed Holmes, shading his eyes. "Yes, I think we had better do as you suggest."

We got off, paid our fare, and the trap rattled back on its way to Leatherhead.

"I thought it as well," said Holmes, as we climbed the stile, "that this fellow should think we had come here as architects, or on some definite business. It may stop his gossip. Good afternoon, Miss Stoner. You see that we have been as good as our word."

Our client of the morning had hurried forward to meet us with a face which spoke her joy. "I have been waiting so eagerly for you," she cried, shaking hands with us warmly. "All has turned out splendidly. Dr. Roylott has gone to town, and it is unlikely that he will be back before evening."

"We have had the pleasure of making the Doctor's acquaintance," said Holmes, and in a few words he sketched out what had occurred. Miss Stoner turned white to the lips as she listened.

"Good heavens!" she cried, "he has followed me, then."

"So it appears."

"He is so cunning that I never know when I am safe from him. What will he say when he returns?"

"He must guard himself, for he may find that there is someone more cunning than himself upon his track. You must lock yourself from him tonight. If he is violent, we shall take you away to your aunt's at Harrow. Now, we must make the best use of our time, so kindly take us at once to the rooms which we are to examine."

The building was of gray, lichen-blotched stone, with a high central portion, and two curving wings, like the claws of a crab, thrown out on each side. In one of these wings the windows were broken, and blocked with wooden boards, while the roof was partly caved in, a picture of ruin.

The central portion was in little better repair, but the right-hand block was comparatively modern, and the blinds in the windows, with the blue smoke curling up from the chimneys, showed that this was where the family resided. Some scaffolding had been erected against the end wall, and the stonework had been broken into, but there were no signs of any workmen at the moment of our visit. Holmes walked slowly up and down the ill-trimmed lawn, and examined with deep attention the outsides of the windows.

"This, I take it, belongs to the room in which you used to sleep, the center one to your sister's, and the one next to the main building to Dr. Roylott's chamber?"

"Exactly so. But I am now sleeping in the middle one."

"Pending the alterations, as I understand. By the way, there does not seem to be any very pressing need for repairs at that end wall."

"There were none. I believe that it was an excuse to move me from my room."

"Ah! that is suggestive. Now, on the other side of this narrow wing runs the corridor from which these three rooms open. There are windows in it, of course?"

"Yes, but very small ones. Too narrow for anyone to pass through."

"As you both locked your doors at night, your rooms were unapproachable from that side. Now, would you have the kindness to go into your room, and to bar your shutters."

Miss Stoner did so, and Holmes, after a careful examination through the open window, endeavored in every way to force the shutter open, but without success. There was no slit through which a knife could be passed to raise the bar. Then with his lens he tested the hinges, but they were of solid iron, built firmly into the massive masonry. "Hum!" said he, scratching his chin in some perplexity, "my theory certainly presents some difficulties. No one could pass these shutters if they were bolted. Well, we shall see if the inside throws any light upon the matter."

A small side door led into the whitewashed corridor from

which the three bedrooms opened. Holmes refused to examine the third chamber, so we passed at once to the second, that in which Miss Stoner was now sleeping, and in which her sister had met her fate. It was a homely little room, with a low ceiling and a gaping fireplace, after the fashion of old country houses. A brown chest of drawers stood in one corner, a narrow white-counterpaned bed in another, and a dressing table on the left-hand side of the window. These articles, with two small wickerwork chairs, made up all the furniture in the room, save for a square of Wilton carpet in the center. The boards around and the paneling of the walls were brown, worm-eaten oak, so old and discolored that it may have dated from the original building of the house. Holmes drew one of the chairs into a corner and sat silent, while his eyes traveled around and around and up and down, taking in every detail of the apartment.

"Where does that bell communicate with?" he asked at last, pointing to a thick bell-rope which hung down beside the bed, the tassel actually lying upon the pillow.

"It goes to the housekeeper's room."

"It looks newer than the other things?"

"Yes, it was only put there a couple of years ago."

"Your sister asked for it, I suppose?"

"No, I never heard of her using it. We used always to get what we wanted for ourselves."

"Indeed, it seemed unnecessary to put so nice a bell-pull there. You will excuse me for a few minutes while I satisfy myself as to this floor." He threw himself down upon his face with his lens in his hand, and crawled swiftly backwards and forwards, examining minutely the cracks between the boards. Then he did the same with the woodwork with which the chamber was paneled. Finally he walked over to the bed and spent some time in staring at it, and in running his eye up and down the wall. Finally he took the bell-rope in his hand and gave it a brisk tug.

"Why, it's a dummy," said he.

"Won't it ring?"

"No, it is not even attached to a wire. This is very interesting. You can see now that it is fastened to a hook just above where the little opening of the ventilator is."

"How very absurd! I never noticed that before."

"Very strange!" muttered Holmes, pulling at the rope. "There are one or two very singular points about this room. For example, what a fool a builder must be to open a ventilator in another room, when, with the same trouble, he might have communicated with the outside air!"

"That is also quite modern," said the lady.

"Done about the same time as the bell-rope?" remarked Holmes.

"Yes, there were several little changes carried out about that time."

"They seem to have been of a most interesting character— dummy bell-ropes, and ventilators which do not ventilate. With your permission, Miss Stoner, we shall now carry our researches into the inner apartment."

Dr. Grimesby Roylott's chamber was larger than that of his stepdaughter, but was as plainly furnished. A camp bed, a small wooden shelf full of books, mostly of a technical character, an armchair beside the bed, a plain wooden chair against the wall, a round table, and a large iron safe were the principal things which met the eye. Holmes walked slowly round and examined each and all of them with the keenest interest.

"What's in here?" he asked, tapping the safe.

"My stepfather's business papers."

"Oh! you have seen inside then?"

"Only once, some years ago. I remember that it was full of papers."

"There isn't a cat in it, for example?"

"No. What a strange idea!"

"Well, look at this!" He took up a small saucer of milk which stood on the top of it.

"No; we don't keep a cat. But there is a cheetah and a baboon."

"Ah, yes, of course! Well, a cheetah is just a big cat, and yet a saucer of milk does not go very far in satisfying its wants, I daresay. There is one point which I should wish to determine." He squatted down in front of the wooden chair, and examined the seat of it with the greatest attention.

"Thank you. That is quite settled," said he, rising and putting his lens in his pocket. "Hello! here is something interesting!"

The object which had caught his eye was a small dog lash hung on one corner of the bed. The lash, however, was curled upon itself, and tied so as to make a loop of whipcord.

"What do you make of that, Watson?"

"It's a common enough lash. But I don't know why it should be tied."

"That is not quite so common, is it? Ah, me! it's a wicked world, and when a clever man turns his brain to crime it is the worst of all. I think that I have seen enough now, Miss Stoner, and, with your permission, we shall walk out upon the lawn."

I had never seen my friend's face so grim, or his brow so dark, as it was when we turned from the scene of his investigation. We had walked several times up and down the lawn, neither Miss Stoner nor myself liking to break in upon his thoughts before he roused himself from his reverie.

"It is very essential, Miss Stoner," said he, "that you should absolutely follow my advice in every respect."

"I shall most certainly do so."

"The matter is too serious for any hesitation. Your life may depend upon your compliance."

"I assure you that I am in your hands."

"In the first place, both my friend and I must spend the night in your room."

Both Miss Stoner and I gazed at him in astonishment.

"Yes, it must be so. Let me explain. I believe that that is the village inn over there?"

"Yes, that is the 'Crown'."

"Very good. Your windows would be visible from there?"

"Certainly."

"You must confine yourself in your room, on pretense of a headache, when your stepfather comes back. Then when you hear him retire for the night, you must open the shutters of your window, undo the hasp, put your lamp there as a signal to us, and then withdraw with everything which you are likely to want into the room which you used to occupy. I have no doubt that, in spite of the repairs, you could manage there for one night."

"Oh, yes, easily."

"The rest you will leave in our hands."

"But what will you do?"

"We shall spend the night in your room, and we shall investigate the cause of this noise which has disturbed you."

"I believe, Mr. Holmes, that you have already made up your mind," said Miss Stoner, laying her hand upon my companion's sleeve.

"Perhaps I have."

"Then for pity's sake tell me what was the cause of my sister's death."

"I should prefer to have clearer proofs before I speak."

"You can at least tell me whether my own thought is correct, and if she died from some sudden fright."

"No, I do not think so. I think that there was probably some more tangible cause. And now, Miss Stoner, we must leave you, for if Dr. Roylott returned and saw us, our journey would be in vain. Goodbye, and be brave, for if you will do what I have told you, you may rest assured that we shall soon drive away the dangers that threaten you."

Sherlock Holmes and I had no difficulty in engaging a bedroom and sitting room at the Crown Inn. They were on the upper floor, and from our window we could command a view of the avenue gate, and of the inhabited wing of Stoke Moran Manor House. At dusk we saw Dr. Grimesby Roylott drive past, his huge form looming up beside the little figure of the lad who drove him. The boy had some slight difficulty in undoing the heavy iron gates, and we heard the hoarse roar of the Doctor's voice, and saw the fury with which he shook his clenched fists at him. The trap drove on, and a few minutes later we saw a sudden light spring up among the trees as the lamp was lit in one of the sitting rooms.

"Do you know, Watson," said Holmes, as we sat together in the gathering darkness, "I have really some scruples as to taking you tonight. There is a distinct element of danger."

"Can I be of assistance?"

"Your presence might be invaluable."

"Then I shall certainly come."

"It is very kind of you."

"You speak of danger. You have evidently seen more in these rooms than was visible to me."

"No, but I fancy that I may have deduced a little more. I imagine that you saw all that I did."

"I saw nothing remarkable save the bell-rope, and what purpose that could answer I confess is more than I can imagine."

"You saw the ventilator, too?"

"Yes, but I do not think that it is such a very unusual thing to have a small opening between two rooms. It was so small a rat could hardly pass through."

"I knew that we should find a ventilator before we ever came to Stoke Moran."

"My dear Holmes!"

"Oh, yes, I did. You remember in her statement she said that her sister could smell Dr. Roylott's cigar. Now, of course that suggests at once that there must be a communication between the two rooms. It could only be a small one, or it would have been remarked upon at the coroner's inquiry. I deduced a ventilator."

"But what harm can there be in that?"

"Well, there is at least a curious coincidence of dates. A ventilator is made, a cord is hung, and a lady who sleeps in the bed dies. Does not that strike you?"

"I cannot as yet see any connection."

"Did you observe anything very peculiar about that bed?"

"No."

"It was clamped to the floor. Did you ever see a bed fastened like that before?"

"I cannot say that I have."

"The lady could not move her bed. It must always be in the same relative position to the ventilator and to the rope—for so we may call it, since it was clearly never meant for a bell-pull."

"Holmes," I cried, "I seem to see dimly what you are hitting at. We are only just in time to prevent some subtle and horrible crime."

"Subtle enough and horrible enough. When a doctor does go wrong he is the first of criminals. He has nerve and he has knowledge. Palmer and Pritchard were among the heads of their profession. This man strikes even deeper, but, I think, Watson, that we shall be able to strike deeper still. But we shall have horrors enough before the night is over: for goodness' sake let us have a quiet pipe, and turn our minds for a few hours to something more cheerful."

About nine o'clock the light among the trees was extinguished, and all was dark in the direction of the Manor House. Two hours passed slowly away, and then, suddenly, just at the stroke of eleven, a single bright light shone out right in front of us.

"That is our signal," said Holmes, springing to his feet; "it comes from the middle window."

As we passed out he exchanged a few words with the landlord, explaining that we were going on a late visit to an acquaintance, and that it was possible that we might spend the night there. A moment later we were out on the dark road, a chill wind blowing in our faces, and one yellow light twinkling in front of us through the gloom to guide us on our somber errand.

There was little difficulty in entering the grounds, for unrepaired breaches gaped in the old park wall. Making our way among the trees, we reached the lawn, crossed it, and were about to enter through the window, when out from a clump of laurel bushes there darted what seemed to be a hideous and distorted child, who threw itself on the grass with writhing limbs, and then ran swiftly across the lawn into the darkness.

"My God!" I whispered, "did you see it?"

Holmes was for the moment as startled as I. His hand closed like a vice upon my wrist in his agitation. Then he broke into a low laugh, and put his lips to my ear.

"It is a nice household," he murmured, "that is the baboon."

I had forgotten the strange pets which the doctor affected. There was a cheetah, too; perhaps we might find it upon our shoulders at any moment. I confess that I felt easier in my mind when, after following Holmes's example and slipping off my shoes, I found myself inside the bedroom. My companion noiselessly closed the shutters, moved the lamp on to the table, and cast his eyes round the room. All was as we had seen it in the daytime. Then creeping up to me and making a trumpet of his hand, he whispered into my ear again so gently that it was all that I could do to distinguish the words:

"The least sound would be fatal to our plans."

I nodded to show that I had heard.

"We must sit without a light. He would see it through the ventilator."

I nodded again.

"Do not go to sleep; your very life may depend upon it. Have your pistol ready in case we should need it. I will sit on the side of the bed, and you in that chair."

I took out my revolver and laid it on the corner of the table.

Holmes had brought up a long thin cane, and this he placed upon the bed beside him. By it he laid the box of matches and the stump of a candle. Then he turned down the lamp and we were left in darkness.

How shall I ever forget that dreadful vigil? I could not hear a sound, not even the drawing of a breath, and yet I knew that my companion sat open-eyed, within a few feet of me, in the same state of nervous tension in which I was myself.

The shutters cut off the least ray of light, and we waited in absolute darkness. From outside came the occasional cry of a nightbird, and once at our very window a long drawn, cat-like whine, which told us that the cheetah was indeed at liberty. Far away we could hear the deep tones of the parish clock, which boomed out every quarter of an hour. How long they seemed, those quarters! Twelve o'clock, and one, and two, and three, and still we sat waiting silently for whatever might befall.

Suddenly there was the momentary gleam of a light up in the direction of the ventilator, which vanished immediately, but was succeeded by a strong smell of burning oil and heated metal. Someone in the next room had lit a dark lantern. I heard a gentle sound of movement, and then all was silent once more, though the smell grew stronger. For half an hour I sat with straining ears. Then suddenly another sound became audible—a very gentle, soothing sound, like that of a small jet of steam escaping continually from a kettle. The instant that we heard it, Holmes sprang from the bed, struck a match, and lashed furiously with his cane at the bell-pull.

"You see it, Watson?" he yelled. "You see it?"

But I saw nothing. At the moment when Holmes struck the light I heard a low, clear whistle, but the sudden glare flashing into my weary eyes made it impossible for me to tell what it was at which my friend lashed so savagely. I could, however, see that his face was deadly pale, and filled with horror and loathing.

He had ceased to strike, and was gazing up at the ventilator, when suddenly there broke from the silence of the night the most horrible cry to which I have ever listened. It swelled up louder and louder, a hoarse yell of pain and fear and anger all mingled in the one dreadful shriek. They say that away down in the village, and even in the distant parsonage, that cry raised the sleepers from their beds. It struck cold to our hearts, and I stood gazing at Holmes, and he at me, until the last echoes of it had died away into the silence from which it rose.

"What can it mean?" I gasped.

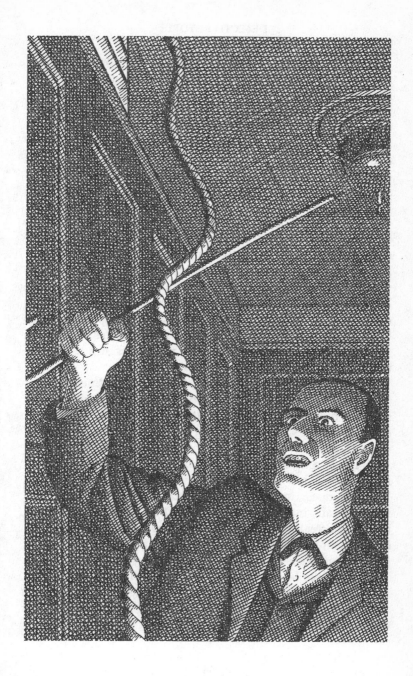

"It means that it is all over," Holmes answered. "And perhaps, after all, it is for the best. Take your pistol, and we shall enter Dr. Roylott's room."

With a grave face he lit the lamp, and led the way down the corridor. Twice he struck at the chamber door without any reply from within. Then he turned the handle and entered, I at his heels, with the cocked pistol in my hand.

It was a singular sight which met our eyes. On the table stood a dark lantern with the shutter half open, throwing a brilliant beam of light upon the iron safe, the door of which was ajar. Beside this table, on the wooden chair, sat Dr. Grimesby Roylott, clad in a long gray dressing gown, his bare ankles protruding beneath, and his feet thrust into red heelless Turkish slippers. Across his lap lay the short stock with the long lash which we had noticed during the day. His chin was cocked upwards, and his eyes were fixed in a dreadful rigid stare at the corner of the ceiling. Round his brow he had a peculiar yellow band, with brownish speckles, which seemed to be bound tight round his head. As we entered he made neither sound nor motion.

"The band! the speckled band!" whispered Holmes.

I took a step forward: in an instant his strange headgear began to move, and there reared itself from among his hair the squat diamond-shaped head and puffed neck of a loathsome serpent.

"It is a swamp adder!" cried Holmes—"the deadliest snake in India. He has died within ten seconds of being bitten. Violence does, in truth, recoil upon the violent, and the schemer falls into the pit which he digs for another. Let us thrust this creature back into its den, and we can then remove Miss Stoner to some place of shelter, and let the county police know what has happened."

As he spoke he drew the dog whip swiftly from the dead man's lap, and throwing the noose round the reptile's neck, he drew it from its horrid perch, and carrying it at arm's length, threw it into the iron safe, which he closed upon it.

*

Such are the true facts of the death of Dr. Grimesby Roylott, of Stoke Moran. It is not necessary that I should prolong a narrative which has already run to too great a length, by telling how we broke the sad news to the terrified girl, how we conveyed her by the morning train to the care of her good aunt at Harrow, of how the slow process of official inquiry came to the conclusion that the Doctor met his fate while indiscreetly playing with a dangerous pet. The little which I had yet to learn of the case was told me by Sherlock Holmes as we traveled back next day.

"I had," said he, "come to an entirely erroneous conclusion, which shows, my dear Watson, how dangerous it always is to reason from insufficient data. The presence of the gypsies, and the use of the word 'band', which was used by the poor girl, no doubt, to explain the appearance which she had caught a horrid glimpse of by the light of her match, were sufficient to put me upon an entirely wrong scent. I can only claim the merit that I instantly reconsidered my position when, however, it became clear to me that whatever danger threatened an occupant of the room could not come either from the window or the door. My attention was speedily drawn as I have already remarked to you, to this ventilator, and to the bell-rope which hung down to the bed. The discovery that this was a dummy, and that the bed was clamped to the floor, instantly gave rise to the suspicion that the rope was there as a bridge for something passing through the hole, and coming to the bed. The idea of a snake instantly occurred to me, and when I coupled it with my knowledge that the Doctor was furnished with a supply of creatures from India, I felt that I was probably on the right track. The idea of using a form of poison which could not possibly be discovered by any chemical test was just such a one as would occur to a clever and ruthless man who had an Eastern training. The rapidity with which such a poison would take effect would also, from his point of view, be an advantage. It would be a sharp-eyed coroner indeed who could distinguish the two little dark punctures which would show where the poison fangs had done their work. Then I thought of the whistle. Of course, he must recall the snake before the morning light revealed it to the victim. He had trained it, probably by the use of the milk which we saw, to return to him when summoned. He would put it through the ventilator at the hour that he thought best, with the certainty that it would crawl down the rope, and land on the bed. It might or might not bite the occupant, perhaps she might escape every night for a week, but sooner or later she must fall a victim.

"I had come to these conclusions before ever I had entered his room. An inspection of his chair showed me that he had been in the habit of standing on it, which, of course, would be necessary in order that he should reach the ventilator. The sight of the safe, the saucer of milk, and the loop of whipcord were really enough to finally dispel any doubts which may have remained. The metallic clang heard by Miss Stoner was obviously caused by her stepfather hastily closing the door of his safe upon its terrible occupant. Having once made up my mind, you know the steps which I took in order to put the matter to the proof. I heard the creature hiss, as I have no doubt that you did also, and I instantly lit the light and attacked it."

"With the result of driving it through the ventilator."

"And also with the result of causing it to turn upon its master at the other side. Some of the blows of my cane came home, and roused its snakish temper, so that it flew upon the first person it saw. In this way I am no doubt indirectly responsible for Dr. Grimesby Roylott's death, and I cannot say that it is likely to weigh very heavily upon my conscience."

COLD MONEY

ELLERY QUEEN

*The stolen money, the secret hiding place, the brutal death in a hotel
room . . . classic ingredients. The sharp-eyed detective Ellery Queen
runs his hand over the dead man's cheek and instantly deduces the
identity of the killer. How does he do it?*

*All the clues are there in front of us, in the pure detective style,
but it's not till we reach the end that we see how cleverly the author
has outwitted us.*

THE HOTEL CHANCELLOR in midtown New York is not
likely to forget the two visits of Mr. Philly Mullane. The
first time Mullane registered at the Chancellor, under
the name of Winston F. Parker, an alert house detective
spotted him and, under the personal direction of Inspector
Richard Queen, Philly was carried out of Room 913,
struggling and in bracelets, to be tried, convicted, and
sentenced to ten years for a Manhattan payroll robbery. The
second time—ten years later—he was carried out neither
struggling nor manacled, inasmuch as he was dead.

The case really began on a blacktop county road east of
Route 7 in the Berkshire foothills, when Mullane sapped his
pal Mikie the Waiter over the left ear and tossed him out of
their getaway car, thereby increasing the split from thirds to

halves. Mullane was an even better mathematician than that. Five miles farther north, he administered the same treatment to Pittsburgh Patience, which left him sole proprietor of their $62,000 haul. Mikie and Patience were picked up by Connecticut state police; the Waiter was speechless with rage, which could not be said of Patience, a lady of inspired vocabulary. Three weeks later Philly Mullane was smoked out of the Chancellor room where he had been sulking. The payroll was absent—in those three weeks the $62,000 had vanished. He had not blown the money in, for the checkback showed that he had made for the New York hotel immediately on ditching his confederates.

Question: Where had Mullane stashed the loot?

Everyone wanted to know. In the case of Pittsburgh Patience and Mikie the Waiter, their thirst for information had to go unsatisfied; they drew ten-year sentences, too. As for the police, for all their success in locating the stolen banknotes, they might as well have gone up the river with Mullane and his ex-associates.

They tried everything on Mullane, including a planted cellmate. But Mullane wasn't talking, even in his sleep.

The closest they came was in the sixth year of Philly's stretch. In July of that year, in the exercise yard, Philly let out a yell that he had been stabbed, and he collapsed. The weapon which had stabbed him was the greatest killer of all, and when he regained consciousness in the infirmary the prison doctor named it for him. It was his heart.

"My pumper?" Mullane said incredulously. "Me?" And then he looked scared, and he said in a weak voice, "I want to see the Warden."

The Warden came at once; he was a kindly man who wished his rough flock well, but he had been waiting for this moment for over five years. "Yes, Mullane?" the Warden said.

"About that sixty-two grand," whispered Philly.

"Yes, Mullane?" the Warden said.

"I never been a Boy Scout, God knows—"

"Yes, He does," said the Warden.

"That's what I mean, Warden. I mean, I figure I can't take it with me, and maybe I can cut down on that book He's keeping on me upstairs. I guess I better tell you where I stashed that dough. The doc tells me I'm going to die—"

But the prison doctor was young and full of Truth and other ideals, and he interrupted indignantly, "I said *eventually*. Not now, Mullane! You may not get another attack for years."

"Oh?" said Philly in a remarkably strong voice. "Then what am I worried about?" And he grinned at the Warden and turned his face to the wall.

The Warden could have kicked both of them.

So everybody settled back to more waiting.

What they were waiting for was Mullane's release. They had plenty of time—the law, Patience, the Waiter, and Mullane most of all. Having behaved themselves as guests of the state, Patience and Mikie got out in something over seven years, and they went their respective ways. Mullane's silence stuck him for the limit.

The day he was released the Warden said to him, "Mullane, you'll never get away with that money. And even if you should, nobody ever gets anything out of money that doesn't belong to him."

"I figure I've earned it, Warden," said Philly Mullane with a crooked smile. "At that, it only comes to a measly sixty-two hundred a year."

"What about your heart?"

"Ah, that doc was from hunger."

Of course, they put a twenty-four hour tail on him. And they lost him. Two headquarters detectives were demoted because of it. When he was found ten days later he had been dead about fifteen minutes.

A long memory and a smart bit of skull work on the part of one of the Hotel Chancellor's house dicks, Blauvelt, were responsible for the quick discovery of the body. Blauvelt had been on a two-week vacation. When he returned to duty, the hotel staff was yakking about a guest named Worth who had checked in nine days before and had not left his room since.

The only ones who had seen him were the room service people—he had all his meals served in his rooms—the chambermaid, and a few bellboys. They reported that he kept his door not only locked day and night, but on the chain. The room was 913, and a desk clerk recalled that Worth had insisted on that room and no other.

"I only came on the job this morning, so I haven't been able to get a look at him," Blauvelt said over the phone to police headquarters, "but from what they tell me, except for a change in the color of his hair and a couple inches in height, which could be elevators, he answers the description. Inspector, if this Worth ain't Philly Mullane hiding out I'll get me a job in the Sanitation Department."

"Nice going, Blauvelt. We'll be right over." Inspector Queen hung up and said admiringly, "Same hotel, same room. You've got to hand it to him—" But then he stopped.

"Exactly," said Ellery, who had been listening on the extension. He remembered the case as one of his father's pet bogies. "It's too smart. Unless that's where he hid the money in the first place."

"But Ellery, that room at the Chancellor was searched when we grabbed Mullane off ten years ago!"

"Not the super deluxe type search I recommend in such cases," mourned Ellery. "Remember how cleverly Mullane led you to believe he'd buried the money during his getaway? He had you digging up half the cornfields in Connecticut! Dad, it's been in that room at the Chancellor all this time."

So they went up to the Chancellor with Sergeant Velie and a couple of precinct men and Blauvelt unlocked the door of 913 with his passkey. The door was off the chain, the reason for which became immediately clear when they saw that Mullane had been murdered.

The precinct men went scurrying, and Sergeant Velie got busy on the phone.

Mullane was in a chair at the writing desk in a corner of the bedroom, his face and arms on the desk. He had been cracked on the back of the head with some heavy object which a quick

examination told them was not there. From the contusion, the Inspector guessed it had been a hammer.

"But this wound doesn't look as if the blow was hard enough to have caused death," frowned Ellery.

"Mullane's ticker went bad in prison," said his father. "Bad heart, hard blow—curtains."

Ellery looked around. The room had not yet been made up for the day and it was in some disorder. He began to amble, mumbling to himself. "Wouldn't have hidden it in a piece of furniture—they're moved around in hotels all the time . . . In *nothing* removable . . . Walls and ceiling tinted plaster—would mean replastering, duplicating the tint . . . too risky . . . " He got down on all fours and began crawling about.

The Inspector was at the desk. "Blauvelt. Help me sit him up."

The body was still warm and the house detective had to hold on to keep it from collapsing. Mullane's dressing-gown sleeves and collar were a mess of wet blue ink. He had been writing a note of some kind and in falling forward had upset the ink bottle.

The Inspector looked around for a towel, but there was none in the bedroom.

"Velie, get some used towels from the bathroom. Maybe we can sop up enough of this wet ink to make out what Mullane was writing!"

"No used towels in here," called the Sergeant from the bathroom.

"Then get clean ones, you dimwit!"

Velie came out with some unused towels, and Inspector Queen went to work on the note. He worked for five minutes, delicately. But all he could show for it were three shaky words: *Money hidden in* . . . The rest was blotted beyond recall.

"Why would he write where the dough was stashed?" wondered Blauvelt, continuing to embrace Mullane.

"Because after he got up this morning," snapped the Inspector, "he must have felt a heart attack coming on. When he got his attack in prison, he almost spilled to the Warden.

This time it probably scared him so much he sat right down and wrote the hiding place of the money. Then he slumped forward, unconscious or dying. Killer got in—maybe thought he was dozing—finished him off, read the note before the ink soaked all the way in—"

"And found the loot," said Ellery from under the bed. "It's gone, Dad."

So Blauvelt let Mullane go and they all got down on their faces and saw the neat hole in the floor, under the rug, with an artistically fitted removable board, where the payroll had lain for ten years. The hole was empty.

When they got to their feet, Ellery was no longer with them. He was stooping over what was left of Mullane.

"Ellery, what are you *doing*?" exclaimed Inspector Queen.

Even Sergeant Velie looked repelled. Ellery was running his palm over the dead man's cheeks with tenderness.

"Nice," he said.

"*Nice!*"

"Nice smooth shave he took this morning. You can still see traces of talcum powder."

Blauvelt's mouth was open.

"You want to learn something, Blauvelt?" said Sergeant Velie with a nudge that doubled the house detective up. "Now it gives a great big deduction."

"Certainly does," grinned Ellery. "It gives the killer of Philly Mullane."

The Sergeant opened his mouth.

"Shut up, Velie," said Inspector Queen. "Well?"

"Because if Mullane shaved this morning," asked Ellery, "where did he do it, Sergeant?"

"Okay, I bite," said Velie. "Where?"

"Where every man shaves, Sergeant—in the bathroom. Ever shave in the bathroom without using a towel?"

"All right, Ellery, so Mullane used a towel," said the Inspector impatiently. "So what?"

"So where is it? When you asked Velie to get one from the bathroom to sop up the ink, Dad, he said *there were no used towels in there.* And there are no towels at all in the bedroom here. What did Velie bring you from the bathroom? Some *unused* towels. In other words, after Mullane shaved this morning, *someone took the dirty towels away and replaced them with clean ones.* And this is a hotel, and Mullane, who always kept the door on the chain, had obviously let someone in . . ."

"*The chambermaid!*"

"Has to be. Mullane let the chambermaid in this morning, as usual, she got to work in the bathroom—and she never did get to the bedroom, as you can see. Why? It can only be because while she was cleaning up in the bathroom Mullane got his heart attack!

"It was the chambermaid who struck Mullane on the back of the head with the hammer she'd brought in with her— waiting for a chance to use it, as she's probably waited every morning for the last nine days.

"It was the chambermaid who read Mullane's message and scooped the money out of the hole in the floor."

"But to have come in with a hammer—she must have planned this, she must have known who he was!"

"Right, Dad. So I think you'll find, when you catch up with her, that the homicidal chambermaid is your old friend, Pittsburgh Patience, with a few alterations in her appearance. Patience suspected all along where Mullane had hidden the money, and as soon as she was out of stir three years ago she got herself a job on the Chancellor housekeeping staff . . . and waited for her old pal to show up!"

THE ADVENTURE OF THE EGYPTIAN TOMB

AGATHA CHRISTIE

Together with Conan Doyle, the name of Agatha Christie is known wherever and in whatever language detective stories are enjoyed. She was a phenomenon: a bestseller for the best part of this century, the author of the longest-running play (The Mousetrap) *ever to be staged, she created not one but two famous detectives, Hercule Poirot and Miss Marple.*

In this story we are with Poirot as he and Captain Hastings tackle a series of mysterious deaths that follow the discovery of an Egyptian tomb. Can there really be a curse that strikes from four thousand years ago? And if not, then what—or who—can possibly be the killer?

I HAVE ALWAYS CONSIDERED that one of the most thrilling and dramatic of the many adventures I have shared with Poirot was that of our investigation into the strange series of deaths which followed upon the discovery and opening of the Tomb of King Men-her-Ra.

Hard upon the discovery of the Tomb of Tutankh-Amen by Lord Carnarvon, Sir John Willard and Mr. Bleibner of New York, pursuing their excavations not far from Cairo, in the vicinity of the Pyramids of Gizeh, came unexpectedly on a series of funeral chambers. The greatest interest was aroused by their discovery. The Tomb appeared to be that of King Men-her-Ra, one of those shadowy kings of the Eighth Dynasty, when the Old Kingdom was falling to decay. Little was known about this period, and the discoveries were fully reported in the newspapers.

An event soon occurred which took a profound hold on the public mind. Sir John Willard died quite suddenly of heart failure.

The more sensational newspapers immediately took the opportunity of reviving all the old superstitious stories connected with the ill luck of certain Egyptian treasures. The unlucky Mummy at the British Museum, that hoary old chestnut, was dragged out with fresh zest, was quietly denied by the Museum, but nevertheless enjoyed all its usual vogue.

A fortnight later Mr. Bleibner died of acute blood poisoning, and a few days afterwards a nephew of his shot himself in New York. The "Curse of Men-her-Ra" was the talk of the day, and the magic power of dead-and-gone Egypt was exalted to a fetish point.

It was then that Poirot received a brief note from Lady Willard, widow of the dead archaeologist, asking him to go and see her at her house in Kensington Square. I accompanied him.

Lady Willard was a tall, thin woman, dressed in deep mourning. Her haggard face bore eloquent testimony to her recent grief.

"It is kind of you to have come so promptly, Monsieur Poirot."

"I am at your service, Lady Willard. You wished to consult me?"

"You are, I am aware, a detective, but it is not only as a detective that I wish to consult you. You are a man of original views, I know, you have imagination, experience of the world; tell me, Monsieur Poirot, what are your views on the supernatural?"

Poirot hesitated for a moment before he replied. He seemed to be considering. Finally he said:

"Let us not misunderstand each other, Lady Willard. It is not a general question that you are asking me there. It has a personal application, has it not? You are referring obliquely to the death of your late husband?"

"That is so," she admitted.

"You want me to investigate the circumstances of his death?"

"I want you to ascertain for me exactly how much is newspaper chatter, and how much may be said to be founded on fact? Three deaths, Monsieur Poirot—each one explicable taken by itself, but taken together surely an almost unbelievable coincidence, and all within a month of the opening of the tomb! It may be mere superstition, it may be some potent curse from the past that operates in ways undreamed of by modern science. The fact remains—three deaths! And I am afraid, Monsieur Poirot, horribly afraid. It may not yet be the end."

"For whom do you fear?"

"For my son. When the news of my husband's death came I was ill. My son, who has just come down from Oxford, went out there. He brought the—the body home, but now he has gone out again, in spite of my prayers and entreaties. He is so fascinated by the work that he intends to take his father's place and carry on the system of excavations. You may think me a foolish, credulous woman, but, Monsieur Poirot, I am afraid. Supposing that the spirit of the dead King is not yet appeased? Perhaps to you I seem to be talking nonsense—"

"No, indeed, Lady Willard," said Poirot quickly. "I, too, believe in the force of superstition, one of the greatest forces the world has ever known."

I looked at him in surprise. I should never have credited Poirot with being superstitious. But the little man was obviously in earnest.

"What you really demand is that I shall protect your son? I will do my utmost to keep him from harm."

"Yes, in the ordinary way, but against an occult influence?"

"In volumes of the Middle Ages, Lady Willard, you will find many ways of counteracting black magic. Perhaps they knew more than we moderns with all our boasted science. Now let us come to facts, that I may have guidance. Your husband had always been a devoted Egyptologist, hadn't he?"

"Yes, from his youth upwards. He was one of the greatest living authorities upon the subject."

"But Mr. Bleibner, I understand, was more or less of an amateur?"

"Oh, quite. He was a very wealthy man who dabbled freely in any subject that happened to take his fancy. My husband managed to interest him in Egyptology, and it was his money that was so useful in financing the expedition."

"And the nephew? What do you know of his tastes? Was he with the party at all?"

"I do not think so. In fact I never knew of his existence till I read of his death in the paper. I do not think he and Mr. Bleibner can have been at all intimate. He never spoke of having any relations."

"Who are the other members of the party?"

"Well, there's Dr. Tosswill, a minor official connected with the British Museum; Mr. Schneider of the Metropolitan Museum in New York; a young American secretary; Dr. Ames, who accompanies the expedition in his professional capacity; and Hassan, my husband's devoted native servant."

"Do you remember the name of the American secretary?"

"Harper, I think, but I cannot be sure. He had not been with Mr. Bleibner very long, I know. He was a very pleasant young fellow."

"Thank you, Lady Willard."

"If there is anything else—"

"For the moment, nothing. Leave it now in my hands, and be assured that I will do all that is humanly possible to protect your son."

They were not exactly reassuring words, and I observed Lady Willard wince as he uttered them. Yet, at the same time, the fact that he had not pooh-poohed her fears seemed in itself to be a relief to her.

For my part I had never before suspected that Poirot had so

deep a vein of superstition in his nature. I tackled him on the subject as we went homeward. His manner was grave and earnest.

"But yes, Hastings. I believe in these things. You must not underrate the force of superstition."

"What are we going to do about it?"

"*Toujours pratique*, the good Hastings! *Eh bien*, to begin with we are going to cable to New York for fuller details of young Mr. Bleibner's death."

He duly sent off his cable. The reply was full and precise. Young Rupert Bleibner had been in low water for several years. He had been a beachcomber and a remittance man in several South Sea islands, but had returned to New York two years ago, where he had rapidly sunk lower and lower. The most significant thing, to my mind, was that he had recently managed to borrow enough money to take him to Egypt. "I've a good friend there I can borrow from," he had declared. Here, however, his plans had gone awry. He had returned to New York cursing his skinflint of an uncle who cared more for the bones of dead-and-gone kings than his own flesh and blood. It was during his sojourn in Egypt that the death of Sir John Willard had occurred. Rupert had plunged once more into his life of dissipation in New York and then, without warning, he had committed suicide, leaving behind him a letter which contained some curious phrases. It seemed written in a sudden fit of remorse. He referred to himself as a leper and an outcast, and the letter ended by declaring that such as he were better dead.

A shadowy theory leapt into my brain. I had never really believed in the vengeance of a long dead Egyptian king. I saw here a more modern crime. Supposing this young man had decided to do away with his uncle—preferably by poison. By mistake, Sir John Willard receives the fatal dose. The young man returns to New York, haunted by his crime. The news of his uncle's death reaches him. He realizes how unnecessary his crime has been, and stricken with remorse takes his own life.

I outlined my solution to Poirot. He was interested.

"It is ingenious what you have thought of there—decidedly it is ingenious. It may even be true. But you leave out of count the fatal influence of the Tomb."

I shrugged my shoulders.

"You still think that has something to do with it?"

"So much so, *mon ami*, that we start for Egypt tomorrow."

"What?" I cried, astonished.

"I have said it." An expression of conscious heroism spread over Poirot's face. Then he groaned. "But oh," he lamented, "the sea! The hateful sea!"

It was a week later. Beneath our feet was the golden sand of the desert. The hot sun poured down overhead. Poirot, the picture of misery, wilted by my side. The little man was not a good traveler. Our four days' voyage from Marseilles had been one long agony to him. He had landed at Alexandria the wraith of his former self, even his usual neatness had deserted him. We had arrived in Cairo and had driven out at once to the Mena House Hotel, right in the shadow of the Pyramids.

The charm of Egypt had laid hold of me. Not so Poirot. Dressed precisely the same as in London, he carried a small clothes brush in his pocket and waged an unceasing war on the dust which accumulated on his dark apparel.

"And my boots," he wailed. "Regard them, Hastings. My boots, of the neat patent leather, usually so smart and shining. See, the sand is inside them, which is painful, and outside them, which outrages the eyesight. Also the heat, it causes my moustaches to become limp—but limp!"

"Look at the Sphinx," I urged. "Even I can feel the mystery and the charm it exhales."

Poirot looked at it discontentedly.

"It has not the air happy," he declared. "How could it, half-buried in sand in that untidy fashion. Ah, this cursed sand!"

"Come, now, there's a lot of sand in Belgium," I reminded him, mindful of a holiday spent at Knocke-sur-mer in the midst of *"Les dunes impeccables"* as the guidebook had phrased it.

"Not in Brussels," declared Poirot. He gazed at the Pyramids thoughtfully. "It is true that they, at least, are of a shape solid and geometrical, but their surface is of an unevenness most unpleasing. And the palm trees, I like them not. Not even do they plant them in rows!"

I cut short his lamentations, by suggesting that we should start for the camp. We were to ride there on camels, and the beasts were patiently kneeling, waiting for us to mount, in charge of several picturesque boys headed by a voluble dragoman.

I pass over the spectacle of Poirot on a camel. He started by groans and lamentations and ended by shrieks, gesticulations and invocations to the Virgin Mary and every Saint in the calendar. In the end, he descended ignominiously and finished the journey on a diminutive donkey. I must admit that a trotting camel is no joke for the amateur. I was stiff for several days.

At last we neared the scene of the excavations. A sunburned man with a gray beard, in white clothes and wearing a helmet, came to meet us.

"Monsieur Poirot and Captain Hastings? We received your cable. I'm sorry that there was no one to meet you in Cairo. An unforeseen event occurred which completely disorganized our plans."

Poirot paled. His hand, which had stolen to his clothes brush, stayed its course.

"Not another death?" he breathed.

"Yes."

"Sir Guy Willard?" I cried.

"No, Captain Hastings. My American colleague, Mr. Schneider."

"And the cause?" demanded Poirot.

"Tetanus."

I blanched. All around me I seemed to feel an atmosphere of evil, subtle and menacing. A horrible thought flashed across me. Supposing I were next?

"*Mon Dieu*," said Poirot, in a very low voice. "I do not

understand this. It is horrible. Tell me, monsieur, there is no doubt that it was tetanus?"

"I believe not. But Dr. Ames will tell you more than I can do."

"Ah, of course, you are not the doctor."

"My name is Tosswill."

This, then, was the British expert described by Lady Willard as being a minor official at the British Museum. There was something at once grave and steadfast about him that took my fancy.

"If you will come with me," continued Dr. Tosswill. "I will take you to Sir Guy Willard. He was most anxious to be informed as soon as you should arrive."

We were taken across the camp to a large tent. Dr. Tosswill lifted up the flap and we entered. Three men were sitting inside.

"Monsieur Poirot and Captain Hastings have arrived, Sir Guy," said Tosswill.

The youngest of the three men jumped up and came forward to greet us. There was a certain impulsiveness in his manner which reminded me of his mother. He was not nearly so sunburned as the others, and that fact, coupled with a certain haggardness around the eyes, made him look older than his twenty-two years. He was clearly endeavoring to bear up under a severe mental strain.

He introduced his two companions, Dr. Ames, a capable-looking man of thirty-odd, with a touch of graying hair at the temples, and Mr. Harper, the secretary, a pleasant, lean young man wearing the national insignia of horn-rimmed spectacles.

After a few minutes' desultory conversation the latter went out, and Dr. Tosswill followed him. We were left alone with Sir Guy and Dr. Ames.

"Please ask any questions you want to ask, Monsieur Poirot," said Willard. "We are utterly dumbfounded at this strange series of disasters, but it isn't—it can't be, anything but coincidence."

There was a nervousness about his manner which rather

belied the words. I saw that Poirot was studying him keenly.

"Your heart is really in this work, Sir Guy?"

"Rather. No matter what happens, or what comes of it, the work is going on. Make up your mind to that."

Poirot wheeled around on the other.

"What have you to say to that, *monsieur le docteur*?"

"Well," drawled the doctor, "I'm not for quitting myself."

Poirot made one of those expressive grimaces of his.

"Then, *èvidemment*, we must find out just how we stand. When did Mr. Schneider's death take place?"

"Three days ago."

"You are sure it was tetanus?"

"Dead sure."

"It couldn't have been a case of strychnine poisoning, for instance?"

"No, Monsieur Poirot, I see what you are getting at. But it was a clear case of tetanus."

"Did you not inject antiserum?"

"Certainly we did," said the doctor drily. "Every conceivable thing that could be done was tried."

"Had you the antiserum with you?"

"No. We procured it from Cairo."

"Have there been any other cases of tetanus in the camp?"

"No, not one."

"Are you certain that the death of Mr. Bleibner was not due to tetanus?"

"Absolutely plumb certain. He had a scratch upon his thumb which became poisoned, and septicemia set in. It sounds pretty much the same to a layman, I dare say, but the two things are entirely different."

"Then we have four deaths—all totally dissimilar, one heart failure, one blood poisoning, one suicide and one tetanus."

"Exactly, Monsieur Poirot."

"Are you certain that there is nothing which might link the four together?"

"I don't quite understand you?"

"I will put it plainly. Was any act committed by those four

men which might seem to denote disrespect to the spirit of Men-her-Ra?"

The doctor gazed at Poirot in astonishment.

"You're talking through your hat, Monsieur Poirot. Surely you've not been guyed into believing all that fool talk?"

"Absolute nonsense," muttered Willard angrily.

Poirot remained placidly immovable, blinking a little out of his green cat's eyes.

"So you do not believe it, *monsieur le docteur*?"

"No, sir, I do not," declared the doctor emphatically. "I am a scientific man, and I believe only what science teaches."

"Was there no science then in Ancient Egypt?" asked Poirot softly. He did not wait for a reply, and indeed Dr. Ames seemed rather at a loss for the moment. "No, no, do not answer me, but tell me this. What do the native workmen think?"

"I guess," said Dr. Ames, "that, where white folk lose their heads, natives aren't going to be far behind. I'll admit that they're getting what you might call scared—but they've no cause to be."

"I wonder," said Poirot noncommittally.

Sir Guy leaned forward.

"Surely," he cried incredulously, "you cannot believe in— oh, but the thing's absurd! You can know nothing of Ancient Egypt if you think that."

For answer Poirot produced a little book from his pocket— an ancient tattered volume. As he held it out I saw its title, *The Magic of the Egyptians and Chaldeans*. Then, wheeling around, he strode out of the tent. The doctor stared at me.

"What is his little idea?"

The phrase, so familiar on Poirot's lips, made me smile as it came from another.

"I don't know exactly," I confessed. "He's got some plan of exorcizing the evil spirits, I believe."

I went in search of Poirot, and found him talking to the lean-faced young man who had been the late Mr. Bleibner's secretary.

"No," Mr. Harper was saying, "I've only been six months with the expedition. Yes, I knew Mr. Bleibner's affairs pretty well."

"Can you recount to me anything concerning his nephew?"

"He turned up here one day, not a bad-looking fellow. I'd never met him before, but some of the others had—Ames, I think, and Schneider. The old man wasn't at all pleased to see him. They were at it in no time, hammer and tongs. 'Not a cent,' the old man shouted. 'Not one cent now or when I'm dead. I intend to leave my money to the furtherance of my life's work. I've been talking it over with Mr. Schneider today.' And a bit more of the same. Young Bleibner lit out for Cairo right away."

"Was he in perfectly good health at the time?"

"The old man?"

"No, the young one."

"I believe he did mention there was something wrong with him. But it couldn't have been anything serious, or I should have remembered."

"One thing more, has Mr. Bleibner left a will?"

"So far as we know, he has not."

"Are you remaining with the expedition, Mr. Harper?"

"No, sir, I am not. I'm for New York as soon as I can square up things here. You may laugh if you like, but I'm not going to be this blasted Men-her-Ra's next victim. He'll get me if I stop here."

The young man wiped the perspiration from his brow.

Poirot turned away. Over his shoulder he said with a peculiar smile:

"Remember, he got one of his victims in New York."

"Oh, hell!" said Mr. Harper forcibly.

"That young man is nervous," said Poirot thoughtfully. "He is on the edge, but absolutely on the edge."

I glanced at Poirot curiously, but his enigmatical smile told me nothing. In company with Sir Guy Willard and Dr. Tosswill we were taken around the excavations. The principal finds had been removed to Cairo, but some of the tomb furniture was extremely interesting. The enthusiasm of the young baronet was obvious, but I fancied that I detected a shade of nervousness in his manner as though he could not quite escape from the feeling of menace in the air. As we entered the tent which had been assigned to us, for a wash before joining the evening meal, a tall dark figure in white robes stood aside to let us pass with a graceful gesture and a murmured greeting in Arabic. Poirot stopped.

"You are Hassan, the late Sir John Willard's servant?"

"I served my Lord Sir John, now I serve his son." He took a step nearer to us and lowered his voice. "You are a wise one, they say, learned in dealing with evil spirits. Let the young master depart from here. There is evil in the air around us."

And with an abrupt gesture, not waiting for a reply, he strode away.

"Evil in the air," muttered Poirot. "Yes, I feel it."

Our meal was hardly a cheerful one. The floor was left to Dr. Tosswill, who discoursed at length upon Egyptian antiquities. Just as we were preparing to retire to rest, Sir Guy caught Poirot by the arm and pointed. A shadowy figure was moving amid the tents. It was no human one: I recognized distinctly the dog-headed figure I had seen carved on the walls of the tomb.

My blood froze at the sight.

"*Mon Dieu!*" murmured Poirot, crossing himself vigorously. "Anubis, the jackal-headed, the god of departing souls."

"Someone is hoaxing us," cried Dr. Tosswill, rising indignantly to his feet.

"It went into your tent, Harper," muttered Sir Guy, his face dreadfully pale.

"No," said Poirot, shaking his head, "into that of the Dr. Ames."

The doctor stared at him incredulously; then repeating Dr. Tosswill's words, he cried:

"Someone is hoaxing us. Come, we'll soon catch the fellow."

He dashed energetically in pursuit of the shadowy apparition. I followed him, but, search as we would, we could find no

trace of any living soul having passed that way. We returned, somewhat disturbed in mind, to find Poirot taking energetic measures, in his own way, to ensure his personal safety. He was busily surrounding our tent with various diagrams and inscriptions which he was drawing in the sand. I recognized the five-pointed star or Pentagon many times repeated. As was his wont, Poirot was at the same time delivering an impromptu lecture on witchcraft and magic in general, White magic as opposed to Black, with various references to the Ka and the Book of the Dead thrown in.

It appeared to excite the liveliest contempt in Dr. Tosswill, who drew me aside, literally snorting with rage.

"Balderdash, sir," he exclaimed angrily. "Pure balderdash. The man's an impostor. He doesn't know the difference between the superstitions of the Middle Ages and the beliefs of Ancient Egypt. Never have I heard such a hotch-potch of ignorance and credulity."

I calmed the excited expert, and joined Poirot in the tent. My little friend was beaming cheerfully.

"We can now sleep in peace," he declared happily. "And I can do with some sleep. My head, it aches abominably. Ah, for a good *tisane!*"

As though in answer to prayer, the flap of the tent was lifted and Hassan appeared, bearing a steaming cup which he offered to Poirot. It proved to be camomile tea, a beverage of which he is inordinately fond. Having thanked Hassan and refused his offer of another cup for myself, we were left alone once more. I stood at the door of the tent some time after undressing, looking out over the desert.

"A wonderful place," I said aloud, "and a wonderful work. I can feel the fascination. This desert life, this probing into the heart of a vanished civilization. Surely, Poirot, you, too, must feel the charm?"

I got no answer, and I turned, a little annoyed. My annoyance was quickly changed to concern. Poirot was lying back across the rude couch, his face horribly convulsed. Beside him was the empty cup. I rushed to his side, then dashed out and across the camp to Dr. Ames's tent.

"Dr. Ames!" I cried. "Come at once."

"What's the matter?" said the doctor, appearing in pajamas.

"My friend. He's ill. Dying. The camomile tea. Don't let Hassan leave the camp."

Like a flash the doctor ran to our tent. Poirot was lying as I left him.

"Extraordinary," cried Ames. "Looks like a seizure—or—what did you say about something he drank?" He picked up the empty cup.

"Only I did not drink it!" said a placid voice.

We turned in amazement. Poirot was sitting up on the bed. He was smiling.

"No," he said gently. "I did not drink it. While my good friend Hastings was apostrophizing the night, I took the opportunity of pouring it, not down my throat, but into a little bottle. That little bottle will go to the analytical chemist. No," —as the doctor made a sudden movement—"as a sensible man, you will understand that violence will be of no avail. During Hastings's absence to fetch you, I have had time to put the bottle in safe keeping. Ah, quick, Hastings, hold him!"

I misunderstood Poirot's anxiety. Eager to save my friend, I flung myself in front of him. But the doctor's swift movement had another meaning. His hand went to his mouth, a smell of bitter almonds filled the air, and he swayed forward and fell.

"Another victim," said Poirot gravely, "but the last. Perhaps it is the best way. He has three deaths on his head."

"Dr. Ames?" I cried, stupefied. "But I thought you believed in some occult influence?"

"You misunderstood me, Hastings. What I meant was that I believe in the terrific force of superstition. Once you get it firmly established that a series of deaths are supernatural, you might almost stab a man in broad daylight, and it would still be put down to the curse, so strongly is the instinct of the supernatural implanted in the human race. I suspected from the first that a man was taking advantage of that instinct. The idea came to him, I imagine, with the death of Sir John

Willard. A fury of superstition arose at once. As far as I could see, nobody could derive any particular profit from Sir John's death. Mr. Bleibner was a different case. He was a man of great wealth. The information I received from New York contained several suggestive points. To begin with, young Bleibner was reported to have said he had a good friend in Egypt from whom he could borrow. It was tacitly understood that he meant his uncle, but it seemed to me that in that case he would have said so outright. The words suggest some boon companion of his own. Another thing, he scraped up enough money to take him to Egypt, his uncle refused outright to advance him a penny, yet he was able to pay the return passage to New York. Someone must have lent him the money."

"All that was very thin," I objected.

"But there was more. Hastings, there occur often enough words spoken metaphorically which are taken literally. The opposite can happen too. In this case, words which were meant literally were taken metaphorically. Young Bleibner wrote plainly enough: 'I am a leper,' but nobody realized that he shot himself because he believed that he contracted the dread disease of leprosy."

"What?" I ejaculated.

"It was the clever invention of a diabolical mind. Young Bleibner was suffering from some minor skin trouble; he had lived in the South Sea Islands, where the disease is common enough. Ames was a former friend of his, and a well-known medical man, he would never dream of doubting his word. When I arrived here, my suspicions were divided between Harper and Dr. Ames, but I soon realized that only the doctor could have perpetrated and concealed the crimes, and I learn from Harper that he was previously acquainted with young Bleibner. Doubtless the latter at some time or another had made a will or had insured his life in favor of the doctor. The latter saw his chance of acquiring wealth. It was easy for him to inoculate Mr. Bleibner with the deadly germs. Then the nephew, overcome with despair at the dread news his friend had conveyed to him, shot himself. Mr. Bleibner, whatever his intentions, had made no will. His fortune would pass to his nephew and from him to the doctor."

"And Mr. Schneider?"

"We cannot be sure. He knew young Bleibner too, remember, and may have suspected something, or, again, the doctor may have thought that a further death motiveless and purposeless would strengthen the coils of superstition. Furthermore, I will tell you an interesting psychological fact, Hastings. A murderer has always a strong desire to repeat his successful crime, the performance of it grows upon him. Hence my fears for young Willard. The figure of Anubis you saw tonight was Hassan dressed up by my orders. I wanted to see if I could frighten the doctor. But it would take more than the supernatural to frighten him. I could see that he was not entirely taken in by my pretenses of belief in the occult. The little comedy I played for him did not deceive him. I suspected that he would endeavor to make me the next victim. Ah, but in spite of *la mer maudite*, the heat abominable, and the annoyances of the sand, the little gray cells still functioned!"

Poirot proved to be perfectly right in his premises. Young Bleibner, some years ago, in a fit of drunken merriment, had made a jocular will, leaving "my cigarette-case you admire so much and everything else of which I die possessed which will be principally debts to my good friend Robert Ames who once saved my life from drowning."

The case was hushed up as far as possible, and, to this day, people talk of the remarkable series of deaths in connection with the Tomb of Men-her-Ra as a triumphal proof of the vengeance of a bygone king upon the desecrators of his tomb —a belief which, as Poirot pointed out to me, is contrary to all Egyptian belief and thought.

EMIL AND THE DETECTIVES

ERICH KÄSTNER

Emil and the Detectives *is one of the best children's books ever written. To call Emil and his friends detectives is actually stretching the definition a bit, because there's no doubt in anyone's mind about who the criminal is. But Emil has to track him down himself. He dare not go to the police, because he has painted a mustache on the statue of Grand Duke Charles, and fears arrest himself. However, as he chases the thief through the unfamiliar streets of Berlin, he finds some unexpected friends.*

This extract begins with Emil setting out to visit his grandmother in the city, with some money in his inside pocket.

THE JOURNEY TO BERLIN BEGINS

EMIL TOOK OFF his school cap and said: "Good afternoon, ladies and gentlemen."

A fat lady who had taken off her shoe because it hurt her said to her neighbor, a man who puffed very hard as he breathed: "Children as polite as this one are rare nowadays. When I think of my own childhood, my word, how different things were." As she talked she twiddled her pinched toes in her left stocking. Emil looked on with interest.

Emil had known for a long time that there were people who always said, "My word, how much better things used to be." So he no longer listened when someone said that in the good old days the air had been healthier or that the bulls had been larger. For usually they did not speak the truth, and the people who said these things were the sort who refused to be satisfied with anything for fear that they might be contented.

He felt in the right-hand pocket of his coat and was not happy until he heard the envelope crackle. So far his traveling companions looked trustworthy. They did not look like thieves or murderers. A woman crocheting a shawl sat next to the man who puffed so loudly. At the window next to Emil sat a gentleman in a bowler hat reading a newspaper.

Suddenly he put his paper aside, took some chocolate from his pocket, held it out to Emil and said: "Well, young man, would you like some of this?"

"Thank you so much," said Emil, taking the chocolate. Then he suddenly remembered his manners, so he took off his cap and bowing said: "My name is Emil Tischbein."

The other people in the carriage smiled. The man in turn solemnly raised his bowler hat and said: "Pleased to make your acquaintance, my name is Grundeis."

Then the fat lady who had taken off her left shoe said to Emil: "Does the dry goods merchant Schmidt still live in Neustadt?"

"Yes, indeed," Emil answered. "Do you know him? He has bought the land on which his shop stands."

"Well, then, will you tell him that Frau Jakob from Gross-Grünau wanted to be remembered to him."

"But I'm going to Berlin."

"You can do it when you get back," said Frau Jakob, who was again exercising her toes. She laughed so heartily that her hat slipped over her face.

"Well, well, so you are going to Berlin?" Herr Grundeis asked.

"Yes, my grandmother is meeting me at the flower stand in the Friedrich-Strasse station," Emil answered, feeling in his coat pocket. The envelope crackled, thank goodness it was still there.

"Do you know Berlin?"

"No."

"Well, you *will* be surprised! In Berlin houses which are a hundred stories high have recently been built. They have to tie roofs to the sky so that they will not blow away. . . . And if anyone is in a particular hurry and wants to get to another part of the city they pack him into a box at the post office, put the box into a tube and shoot it like a pneumatic letter to the post office in the part of the city where he wants to go. . . . And if one has money one can go to a bank, get fifty pounds and leave one's brain in exchange. No human being can live longer than two days without a brain, and he can't get it back from the bank unless he pays sixty pounds. Some wonderful medical machines have recently been invented . . ."

"Your brain must be at the bank just now," the man who puffed so loudly said to the man in the bowler hat. Then he added: "Stop talking that nonsense."

Fat Frau Jakob's toes stood still in fear. And the lady who was crocheting the shawl paused as well.

Emil laughed in a forced manner, and the gentleman began a fierce argument. Emil didn't care. So he unpacked his sausage sandwiches, although he had only just had his dinner. As he was eating his third sandwich the train stopped at a big station. Emil could neither see the name of the station nor could he understand what the porter was shouting in front of the window. Most of the passengers left the carriage: the puffing man, the crocheting lady and Frau Jakob. She was almost too late because she couldn't fasten her shoe.

"Well, remember me to Herr Schmidt," she said again. Emil nodded.

And then he and the man with the bowler hat were alone. Emil was not very pleased about this. A strange man who gives away chocolate and tells crazy tales is rather a queer person. Emil wanted to feel his envelope again, but he didn't dare. Instead, as soon as the train started again he went to the washroom, where he took the envelope out of his pocket and counted the money. It was still all there, but he did not know what to do to make the money more safe. Finally an idea occurred to him. He took a pin from the lapel of his coat, stuck it through the banknotes and the envelope and then he finally pinned it to the lining of his suit. "There now," Emil thought, "now nothing can happen to it." And then he went back into the railway carriage.

Herr Grundeis, who had made himself comfortable in a corner of the carriage, was asleep. Emil was glad that he didn't have to talk to him, for he liked looking out of the window. Trees, windmills, factories, cowherds, and waving peasants rushed past and it was pleasant to see them whirling by as though they were on a gramophone record. But after all, one can't stare out of a window for hours on end.

Herr Grundeis went on sleeping and snored a little. Emil would like to have walked up and down, but had he done so he would soon have awakened him, and he didn't want to do this in the least, so he leaned back in the opposite corner of the compartment and watched the sleeping man. Why did he always keep his hat on? He had rather a long face, a tiny black mustache, and a hundred wrinkles around his mouth. His ears were very thin and stuck out away from his head.

Wouf! Emil was startled with fright. He had almost fallen asleep. This he mustn't do under any circumstances. If only someone else had got into the carriage. The train stopped several times but no one came into the carriage. It was only four o'clock and the journey would last more than two hours longer. Emil pinched his legs to keep himself awake. This method was always effective in school when Herr Bremser, the history master, was teaching Emil's class.

For a while this method helped him now. Emil wondered what Pony Hütchen looked like. He could not remember her face at all. He only knew that during the last visit—when she and Grandmother and Aunt Martha had been in Neustadt— she had wanted to box with him. He had, of course, refused, because she was only a flyweight and he was at least a welterweight. It would have been unfair, he had said at the time. And if he had given her an upper cut he would have been obliged to scratch her off the wall afterwards. But she had not stopped nagging him to box with her until Aunt Martha forbade it.

Wouf! he had almost fallen off the seat. Had he been asleep? He pinched his legs again and again. He must have been covered with blue and green bruises already. But despite this fact the pinching did not seem to do any good.

He tried counting buttons. He counted them down and then he counted them up, and then he counted them again, beginning at the lowest one. Counting down there were twenty-three buttons. Counting up there were twenty-four. Emil leaned back, wondering why this could be.

And as he wondered he fell sound asleep.

EMIL GETS OUT AT THE WRONG STATION

When he awoke the train was just beginning to move. He had fallen from the seat in his sleep and found himself lying on the floor of the carriage very much frightened. He didn't quite know why he was frightened. His heart was beating like a steam-hammer. There he was in a railway train and he had almost forgotten where he was. Gradually everything came back to him. Of course: he was going to Berlin. And he had fallen asleep just as the gentleman in the bowler hat had fallen asleep. . . .

Emil sat bolt upright with a jerk, rubbed his eyes and whispered: "Why, he has gone!" His knees were trembling. He got up very slowly, mechanically brushing the dust off his suit as he did so. The next question was: is the money still there? And this question filled him with an indescribable terror.

He stood leaning against the door without moving for a long time. The man whose name was Grundeis had just sat there—eating, sleeping, and snoring. Now he was gone.

Perhaps everything may still be all right. It was silly to fear the worst at once. Just because *he* was traveling to the Friedrich-Strasse station in Berlin it did not mean that everyone was going there. And the money must surely be in its proper place, for he had pinned it securely to his coat and it was safely in an envelope. Slowly and tremblingly, he put his right hand inside his pocket.

The pocket was empty! The money was gone!

Emil burrowed through his pocket with his left hand. In fact he felt in every pocket of his suit, but all to no avail—it was gone—the money was gone.

"Ouch!" Emil took his hand out of his pocket. He withdrew not only his hand, but the pin with which he had fastened the money to his coat. Nothing but the pin was left. And the pin had pricked his left forefinger and it was bleeding.

He wrapped his handkerchief around his finger and cried. Naturally he was not crying because of this tiny bead of blood. Two weeks before he had run into a lamp standard so hard it almost bent over and Emil still had a bump on his forehead. But he had not cried even for a moment.

He was crying about the money. And he was crying because of his mother. Anyone who does not understand this is beyond help, no matter how brave he or she may be. Emil knew how frightfully hard his mother had worked for months to save the seven pounds for his grandmother and for his own journey to Berlin. And hardly had he got into the train before he leaned back in his corner, went to sleep, dreamed a crazy dream, and let that pig of a man steal the money. Wasn't it indeed bad enough to make him cry? What on earth should he do? Get off the train in Berlin and say to his grandmother: "Here I am, but you must know right away that I have no money for you. Not only that, but you will have to give me some money for my fare back to Neustadt!"

That would be impossible. His mother would have saved her money for nothing. Grandmother would not get a penny. He could not stay in Berlin, he could not go back home. And all because of a wicked strange man who gave children chocolate and pretended that he was asleep. And then robbed them! Oh dear, what a dreadful world it was! Emil sobbed.

Emil swallowed the tears that wanted so much to be wept and looked around. If he pulled the emergency cord the train would stop at once. And then a guard would come and another and yet another. And they would all ask: "What has happened? What's the matter?"

"My money has been stolen," Emil would say.

"The next time you'd better look after it properly," they would answer. "Be so good as to get back into the train. What is your name? What is your address? It costs five pounds to pull the emergency cord. The bill will be sent to your home."

In express trains there are corridors so that one can walk from one end of the train to the other until one reaches the compartment where the guard is sitting. Then one can report a theft. But here! in a slow train like this there is no corridor, so one must wait until the train stops at the next station. And in the meantime the man in the bowler hat would have made his escape. Emil didn't even know at what station he had left the train. What time was it, Emil wondered? When would they reach Berlin? Large houses and villas with gay gardens, then tall, dirty red chimney-pots wandered by the train. Probably this was already Berlin. At the next station he must call the guard and tell him everything. And then the guard would notify the police at once.

That meant that, added to everything else, he would be mixed up with the police. So that Constable Jeschke could not, of course, remain silent any longer. Instead, he would be obliged to report officially: "I don't know exactly why, but I don't quite like that schoolboy, Emil Tischbein from Neustadt. He daubs with his chalks on dignified monuments. And then he lets himself be robbed of seven pounds. Perhaps they were not stolen at all? Anyone who is capable of drawing a mustache on a monument is capable of lying. Experience teaches me this much. He has probably buried the money in the woods, or swallowed it so that he can use it to travel to America? There is no point at all in trying to find the thief.

70

Emil Tischbein is the thief. I ask you, Chief of Police, to have him arrested."

This was a terrible thought! He could not even confide in the police!

He took his suitcase down from the rack, put on his cap, stuck the pin back behind the lapel of his coat, and got ready to go. He had not the slightest notion what he would do next, but he could not bear to be in this compartment for more than another five minutes, that was certain.

The train, in the meantime, was slowing down. Emil saw rows of shining tracks outside the window. Then they passed a number of platforms. A few porters ran along next to the carriages.

The train stopped!

Emil looked out of the window and saw a sign high up above the platforms. It said ZOOLOGICAL GARDENS. The doors flew open, people climbed out of the compartments. Other people were waiting with outstretched arms, to give them a warm welcome.

Emil leaned out of the window, looking for the guard. Suddenly he saw a black bowler hat some distance away among the crowd. What if that were the thief? Perhaps after stealing Emil's money he had not left the train but had merely got into another compartment?

In another instant Emil stood on the platform. He hurriedly put down his bag, leapt into the carriage again because he had forgotten the flowers on the luggage rack, then he got out again, picked up his suitcase, and ran as fast as he could toward the exit.

Where was the bowler hat? The boy stumbled around people's legs, hit someone with his suitcase, and ran on. The crowd was getting denser and denser and it was harder and harder to forge a way through.

There! there was the bowler hat! My word, but there was another! Emil could hardly carry his suitcase any farther. He would have preferred to put it down and leave it standing there in the station. But then someone might steal it!

Finally he pushed his way through the crowd so that he was near the bowler hat.

That man might be the thief! Was it he?

No.

There is another one.

No. This man was too short.

Emil wound his way in and out of the crowd like a Red Indian.

There, there!

That was the fellow. Thank goodness! That was Grundeis. He was pushing his way through the barrier and seemed to be in a great hurry.

"Just you wait, you beast," Emil growled. "I'll get you yet!" Then he gave up his ticket, changed his suitcase to his other hand, pressed the flowers under his right arm, and ran down the stairs after the man.

"Now or never!" Emil muttered to himself.

Tram Number 177

Emil would like to have dashed up to the fellow and standing in front of him to have shouted: "Hand over that money!" But the man did not look as though he would reply: "With pleasure, my dear boy. Here it is. I assure you that I will never steal again." The whole affair was not as simple as all that. For the moment the most important thing was not to let the man out of his sight.

Emil hid behind a very fat lady who was walking ahead of him and peered out from behind her. He looked first to the right and then to the left to make sure that the man was still in sight and to see that he did not suddenly run off in another direction. The man, in the meantime, had reached the main entrance to the station and was looking around scanning the crowd as though he was looking for someone. Emil pressed close behind the fat lady, thus getting closer and closer to the man in the bowler hat. What would happen next? Soon he would be obliged to pass the man and then he could no longer keep his presence a secret. Would the lady help him? No, probably she would not believe his story. Then the thief would say: "So sorry, madam, but how can you think such a thing? Do I look as though I were so poor that I must rob little children?" And then all the people standing around would stare at the boy and say: "Really, this is too much! He lies about grown-up people! Nowadays children are altogether too impudent!" Emil's teeth were already chattering.

Fortunately at this moment the man turned his head and stepped out into the open square. The boy jumped behind the door quick as a flash, put down his bag, and peered out of the barred window. My word, how frightfully his arm ached. The thief crossed the road slowly, looked back once more and then walked on, apparently reassured. A Number 177 tram with a trailer turned into the road from a side street at the left. The tram stopped. The man hesitated a moment, then got into the front tramcar and sat down next to a window.

Emil snatched up his bag again, ducked past the door, bolted down the passage, out of another door and into the street. He reached the trailer-car just as the tram was starting. He threw his suitcase onto the platform, climbed after it, pushed it into a corner, stationed himself in front of it, and breathed deeply with relief. Well, so far, so good!

But what next? If the thief jumped off the tram while it was moving the money was lost for good, for Emil could not possibly follow with the suitcase. That would be too dangerous.

The motorcars rushed past the tram honking and squeaking, signaling right and left turns, swinging around corners, while other cars followed immediately behind them. How noisy the traffic was! And there were so many people on the pavements as well! And from every side street came delivery vans, tramcars, and double-decker buses! There were newspaper stands at every corner, and wonderful shop windows filled with flowers and fruit and others filled with books, gold watches, clothes, and silk underwear. And how very, very tall the buildings were.

So this was Berlin.

Emil longed to look at everything in peace. But there was no time for that. In the front tramcar sat a man who had Emil's money, and this man might get off the tram at any moment and disappear in the crowd. Then everything would be hopeless, because out there among the motorcars and the crowd and the buses, one could never find anyone again. Emil looked over the platform railing. What if the fellow had already gone? Then he would be riding on alone, not knowing why he was there or in what direction the tram was carrying him. And his grandmother, in the meantime, was waiting at the flower stand in the Friedrich-Strasse station without the slightest idea that her grandson was journeying to Berlin on tram Number 177, and that he was in serious trouble. The situation was almost unbearable.

The tram stopped for the first time. Emil kept his eye on the forward car. But no one got out. Only a stream of new passengers got into the tram. They pushed by Emil. One man grumbled because the boy's head was in his way.

"Can't you see that other people want to get on?" he growled.

The conductor, who was taking fares inside the tram, pulled the bell-cord. The bell rang and the tram moved on. Emil returned to his corner where he was pushed about. People stepped on his feet. All of a sudden he thought in fright: "Why, I have no money. When the conductor comes out again I must buy a ticket, and if I can't buy one he'll put me off the tram, and then I might as well be buried."

He looked at the people standing near him. Could he pull one of them by the coat and say: "Please lend me some money for my fare?" Oh dear, they all looked so serious. One of them was reading a newspaper, two others were discussing a big bank robbery.

"They dug a tunnel," one of them was saying, "and through it they got into the bank and cleared every penny out of the vaults. The loss probably amounts to several million."

"It will be very difficult to make sure what was actually in the safety-deposit boxes," the other replied, "because people who rent them are not obliged to tell the bank what they have locked up in them."

"Some people might claim that they had lost diamonds worth twenty thousand pounds when, actually, they had only a pile of worthless paper money or a dozen plated spoons in their box." Then they both laughed a little.

"That's just what will happen to me," Emil thought sadly. "When I say that Herr Grundeis stole seven pounds from me, no one will believe me. The thief will say that I am being impertinent and that he only stole three and six. What a horrible muddle."

The conductor came nearer and nearer to the door. Already he was standing in the doorway calling: "Fares! All fares, please!"

He ripped off long white strips of paper and made rows of holes with a ticket-punch. The people on the platform handed him their money and received their ticket in return. "And you?" he asked Emil.

"I have lost my money, sir," Emil said, because no one would believe his story about the theft.

"Lost your money? I've heard that tale before. And where do you want to go?"

"I—I—don't know yet," Emil stuttered.

"I see. Well, then, see that you get off at the next stop and make up your mind where you want to go."

"No, I can't do that. I must stay here, please, sir."

"If I tell you to get off, off you get. Understand?"

"Give the boy a ticket!" said the man who had been reading a newspaper. He handed the conductor a coin. And the conductor gave Emil a ticket and said to the gentleman: "You don't know, you don't, how many boys get on this tram every day and try to make me believe that they have forgotten their money. Then they just laugh at me behind my back."

"This one won't laugh at us," the gentleman answered.

The conductor returned to the inside of the tram.

"Thank you so very, very much, sir," Emil said.

"Oh, that's all right!" the gentleman answered, returning to his newspaper.

Then the tram stopped again. Emil leaned out to see whether the man in the bowler hat would get out. But he could see nothing.

"May I ask you for your address, please?" Emil asked the gentleman.

"Whatever for?"

"So that I can return the money as soon as I have some myself. I'm stopping in Berlin for about a week, so I could bring it around to you. My name is Tischbein. Emil Tischbein, from Neustadt."

"Not at all," the gentleman said; "the fare was a gift, of course. Shall I give you some more?"

"No, indeed," Emil said firmly. "I couldn't accept any more."

And the tram moved on. And then stopped. And then it went on again. Emil read the name of the beautiful wide road. Kaiser Avenue it was called. He was riding on not knowing where he was going. The thief was still sitting in the other tramcar. And perhaps there were other thieves in the tram as well. No one took any notice of Emil. True, a strange gentleman had given him his fare. But now this gentleman was reading his newspaper again!

The city was so large, and Emil was so small. And no one was interested in knowing why he had no money and why he did not know where he was going to get off the tram. Four million people lived in Berlin and not one of them was interested in Emil Tischbein. No one wants to know about other people's troubles. And when anyone says: "I'm most frightfully sorry about that," he does not usually mean anything more than: "Oh, do leave me alone!"

What was going to happen? Emil swallowed hard and felt very unhappy and lonely.

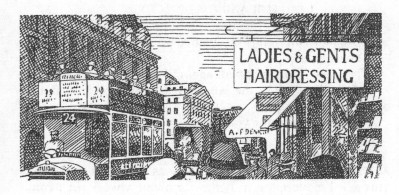

THE INSPIRATION OF
MR. BUDD

DOROTHY L. SAYERS

Sometimes the most unlikely people have the chance to become detectives. Dorothy L. Sayers, who was one of the most popular detective story writers of the century, tells us here about a mild and timid hairdresser. What could a man like him do to capture a brutal murderer? Something, in the end, that only a hairdresser could do.

£500 REWARD

The *Evening Messenger*, ever anxious to further the ends of justice, has decided to offer the above reward to any person who shall give information leading to the arrest of the man, William Strickland, alias Bolton, who is wanted by the police in connection with the murder of the late Emma Strickland at 59, Acacia Crescent, Manchester.

DESCRIPTION OF THE WANTED MAN

The following is the official description of William Strickland: Age 43; height 6ft. 1 or 2; complexion rather dark; hair silver-gray and abundant, may dye same; full gray mustache and beard, may now be clean-shaven; eyes light gray, rather close-set; hawk nose; teeth strong and white, displays them somewhat prominently when laughing, left upper eyetooth stopped with gold; left thumbnail disfigured by recent blow.

Speaks in rather loud voice; quick, decisive manner. Good address.

May be dressed in a gray or dark blue lounge suit, with stand-up collar (size 15) and soft felt hat.

Absconded 5th inst., and may have left, or will endeavor to leave, the country.

Mr. Budd read the description through carefully once again and sighed. It was in the highest degree unlikely that William Strickland should choose his small and unsuccessful saloon, out of all the barber's shops in London, for a haircut or a shave, still less for "dyeing same;" even if he was in London, which Mr. Budd saw no reason to suppose.

Three weeks had gone by since the murder, and the odds were a hundred to one that William Strickland had already left a country too eager with its offer of free hospitality. Nevertheless, Mr. Budd committed the description, as well as he could, to memory. It was a chance—just as the Great Crossword Tournament had been a chance, just as the Ninth Rainbow Ballot had been a chance, and the Bunko Poster

Ballot, and the Monster Treasure Hunt organized by the *Evening Clarion*. Any headline with money in it could attract Mr. Budd's fascinated eye in these lean days, whether it offered a choice between fifty thousand pounds down and ten pounds a week for life, or merely a modest hundred or so.

It may seem strange, in an age of shingling and bingling, Mr. Budd should look enviously at Complete Lists of Prize-winners. Had not the hairdresser across the way, who only last year had eked out his mean ninepences with the yet meaner profits on cheap cigarettes and comic papers, lately bought out the greengrocer next door, and engaged a staff of exquisitely coiffed assistants to adorn his new "Ladies' Hairdressing Department" with its purple and orange curtains, its two rows of gleaming marble basins, and an apparatus like a Victorian chandelier for permanent waving?

Had he not installed a large electric sign surrounded by a scarlet border that ran around and around perpetually, like a kitten chasing its own cometary tail? Was it not his sandwich-man even now patroling the pavement with a luminous announcement of Treatment and Prices? And was there not at this moment an endless stream of young ladies hastening into those heavily perfumed parlors in the desperate hope of somehow getting a shampoo and a wave "squeezed in" before closing time?

If the reception clerk shook a regretful head, they did not think of crossing the road to Mr. Budd's dimly lighted window. They made an appointment four days ahead and waited patiently, anxiously fingering the bristly growth at the back of the neck and the straggly bits behind the ears that so soon got out of hand.

Day after day Mr. Budd watched them flit in and out of the rival establishment, willing, praying even, in a vague, ill-directed manner, that some of them would come over to him; but they never did.

And yet Mr. Budd knew himself to be the finer artist. He had seen shingles turned out from over the way that he would never have countenanced, let alone charged three shillings and sixpence for. Shingles with an ugly hard line at the nape, shingles which were a slander on the shape of a good head or brutally emphasized the weak points of an ugly one; hurried, conscienceless shingles, botched work, handed over on a crowded afternoon to a girl who had only served a three years' apprenticeship and to whom the final mysteries of "tapering" were a sealed book.

And then there was the "tinting"—his own pet subject, which he had studied *con amore*—if only those too-sprightly matrons would come to him! He would gently dissuade them from that dreadful mahogany dye that made them look like metallic robots—he would warn them against that widely advertised preparation which was so incalculable in its effects; he would use the cunning skill which long experience had matured in him—tint them with the infinitely delicate art which conceals itself.

Yet nobody came to Mr. Budd but the navvies and the young loungers and the men who plied their trade beneath the naphtha-flares in Wilton Street.

And why could not Mr. Budd also have burst out into marble and electricity and swum to fortune on the rising tide?

The reason is very distressing, and, as it fortunately has no bearing on the story, shall be told with merciful brevity.

Mr. Budd had a younger brother, Richard, whom he had promised his mother to look after. In happier days Mr. Budd had owned a flourishing business in their native town of Northampton, and Richard had been a bank clerk. Richard had got into bad ways (poor Mr. Budd blamed himself dreadfully for this). There had been a sad affair with a girl, and a horrid series of affairs with bookmakers, and then Richard had tried to mend bad with worse by taking money from the bank. You need to be very much more skillful than Richard to juggle successfully with bank ledgers.

The bank manager was a hard man of the old school: he prosecuted. Mr. Budd paid the bank and the bookmakers, and saw the girl through her trouble while Richard was in prison, and paid their fares to Australia when he came out, and gave them something to start life on.

But it took all the profits of the hairdressing business, and he couldn't face all the people in Northampton anymore, who had known him all his life. So he had run to vast London, the refuge of all who shrink from the eyes of their neighbors, and bought this little shop in Pimlico, which had done fairly well, until the new fashion which did so much for other hairdressing businesses killed it for the lack of capital.

That is why Mr. Budd's eye was so painfully fascinated by headlines with money in them.

He put the newspaper down, and as he did so, caught sight of his own reflection in the glass and smiled, for he was not without a sense of humor. He did not look quite the man to catch a brutal murderer single-handed. He was well on in the middle forties—a trifle paunchy, with fluffy pale hair, getting a trifle thin on top (partly hereditary, partly worry, that was), five feet six at most, and soft-handed, as a hairdresser must be.

Even razor in hand, he would hardly be a match for William Strickland, height six feet one or two, who had so ferociously battered his old aunt to death, so butcherly hacked her limb from limb, so horribly disposed of her remains in the copper. Shaking his head dubiously, Mr. Budd advanced to the door, to cast a forlorn eye at the busy establishment over the way, and nearly ran into a bulky customer who dived in rather precipitately.

"I beg your pardon, sir," murmured Mr. Budd, fearful of alienating ninepence; "just stepping out for a breath of fresh air, sir. Shave, sir?"

The large man tore off his overcoat without waiting for Mr. Budd's obsequious hands.

"Are you prepared to die?" he demanded abruptly.

The question chimed in so alarmingly with Mr. Budd's thoughts about murder that for a moment it quite threw him off his professional balance.

"I beg your pardon, sir," he stammered, and in the same moment decided that the man must be a preacher of some kind. He looked rather like it, with his odd, light eyes, his

82

bush of fiery hair and short, jutting chin-beard. Perhaps he even wanted a subscription. That would be hard, when Mr. Budd had already set him down as ninepence, or, with tip, possibly even a shilling.

"Do you do dyeing?" said the man impatiently.

"Oh!" said Mr. Budd, relieved, "yes, sir, certainly, sir."

A stroke of luck, this. Dyeing meant quite a large sum—his mind soared to seven-and-sixpence.

"Good," said the man, sitting down and allowing Mr. Budd to put an apron about his neck. (He was safely gathered in now—he could hardly dart away down the street with a couple of yards of white cotton flapping from his shoulders.)

"Fact is," said the man, "my young lady doesn't like red hair. She says it's conspicuous. The other ladies in her firm make jokes about it. So, as she's a good bit younger than I am, you see, I like to oblige her, and I was thinking perhaps it could be changed into something quieter, what? Dark brown, now—that's the color she has a fancy for. What do *you* say?"

It occurred to Mr. Budd that the young ladies might consider this abrupt change of coat even funnier than the original color, but in the interests of business he agreed that dark brown would be very becoming and a great deal less noticeable than red. Besides, very likely there was no young lady. A woman, he knew, will say frankly that she wants different colored hair for a change, or just to try, or because she fancies it would suit her, but if a man is going to do a silly thing he prefers, if possible, to shuffle the responsibility on to someone else.

"Very well, then," said the customer, "go ahead. And I'm afraid the beard will have to go. My young lady doesn't like beards."

"A great many young ladies don't, sir," said Mr. Budd. "They're not so fashionable nowadays as they used to be. It's very fortunate that you can stand a clean shave very well, sir. You have just the chin for it."

"Do you think so?" said the man, examining himself a little anxiously. "I'm glad to hear it."

"Will you have the mustache off as well, sir?"

"Well, no—no, I think I'll stick to that as long as I'm allowed to, what?" He laughed loudly, and Mr. Budd approvingly noted well-kept teeth and a gold stopping. The customer was obviously ready to spend money on his personal appearance.

In fancy, Mr. Budd saw this well-off and gentlemanly customer advising all his friends to visit "his man"— "wonderful fellow—wonderful—round at the back of Victoria Station—you'd never find it by yourself—only a little place, but he knows what he's about—I'll write it down for you." It was imperative that there be no fiasco. Hair dyes were awkward things—there had been a case in the paper lately.

"I see you have been using a tint before, sir," said Mr. Budd with respect. "Could you tell me—?"

"Eh?" said the man. "Oh, yes—well, fact is, as I said, my fiancée's a good bit younger than I am. As I expect you can see I began to go gray early—my father was just the same—all our family—so I had it touched up—streaky bits restored, you see. But she doesn't take to the color, so I thought, if I have to dye it at all, why not a color she *does* fancy while we're about it, what?"

It is a common jest among the unthinking that hairdressers are garrulous. This is their wisdom. The hairdresser hears many secrets and very many lies. In his discretion he occupies his unruly tongue with the weather and the political situation, lest, restless with inaction, it plunge unbridled into a mad career of inconvenient candor.

Lightly holding forth upon the caprices of the feminine mind, Mr. Budd subjected his customer's locks to the scrutiny of trained eye and fingers. Never—never in the process of nature could hair of that texture and quality have been red. It was naturally black hair, prematurely turned, as some black hair will turn, to a silvery gray. However that was none of his business. He elicited the information he really needed—the name of the dye formerly used, and noted that he would have to be careful. Some dyes do not mix kindly with other dyes.

Chatting pleasantly, Mr. Budd lathered his customer,

removed the offending beard, and executed a vigorous shampoo, preliminary to the dyeing process. As he wielded the roaring drier, he reviewed Wimbledon, the Silk-tax and the Summer Time Bill—at that moment threatened with sudden strangulation—and passed naturally on to the Manchester murder.

"The police seem to have given it up as a bad job," said the man.

"Perhaps the reward will liven things up a bit," said Mr. Budd, the thought being naturally uppermost in his mind.

"Oh, there's a reward, is there? I hadn't seen that."

"It's in tonight's paper, sir. Maybe you'd like to have a look at it."

"Thanks, I should."

Mr. Budd left the drier to blow the fiery bush of hair at its own wild will for a moment, while he fetched the *Evening Messenger*. The stranger read the paragraph carefully and Mr. Budd, watching him in the glass, after the disquieting manner of his craft, saw him suddenly draw back his left hand, which was resting carelessly on the arm of the chair, and thrust it under the apron.

But not before Mr. Budd had seen it. Not before he had taken conscious note of the horny, misshapen thumbnail. Many people had such an ugly mark, Mr. Budd told himself hurriedly—there was his friend, Bert Webber, who had sliced the top of his thumb right off in a motorcycle chain—his nail looked very much like that.

The man glanced up, and the eyes of his reflection became fixed on Mr. Budd's face with a penetrating scrutiny—a horrid warning that the real eyes were steadfastly interrogating the reflection of Mr. Budd.

"Not but what," said Mr. Budd, "the man is safe out of the country by now, I reckon. They've put it off too late."

The man laughed.

"I reckon they have," he said. Mr. Budd wondered whether many men with smashed left thumbs showed a gold upper eyetooth. Probably there were hundreds of people like that

going around the country. Likewise with silver-gray hair ("may dye same") and aged about forty-three. Undoubtedly.

Mr. Budd folded up the drier and turned off the gas. Mechanically he took a comb and drew it through the hair that never, never in the process of Nature had been that fiery red.

There came back to him, with an accuracy which quite unnerved him, the exact number and extent of the brutal wounds inflicted upon the Manchester victim—an elderly lady, rather stout, she had been. Glancing through the door, Mr. Budd noticed that his rival over the way had closed. The streets were full of people. How easy would it be—

"Be as quick as you can, won't you?" said the man, a little impatiently, but pleasantly enough. "It's getting late. I'm afraid it will keep you over time."

"Not at all, sir," said Mr. Budd. "It's of no consequence—not the least."

No—if he tried to bolt out of the door, his terrible customer would leap upon him, drag him back, throttle his cries, and then with one frightful blow like the one he had smashed his aunt's skull with—

Yet surely Mr. Budd was in a position of advantage. A decided man would do it. He would be out in the street before the customer could disentangle himself from the chair. Mr. Budd began to edge around toward the door.

"What's the matter?" said the customer.

"Just stepping out to look at the time, sir," said Mr. Budd, meekly pausing. (Yet he might have done it then, if he only had the courage to make the first swift step that would give the game away.)

"It's five-and-twenty past eight," said the man, "by tonight's broadcast. I'll pay extra for the overtime."

"Not on any account," said Mr. Budd. Too late now, he couldn't make another effort. He vividly saw himself tripping on the threshold—falling—the terrible fist lifted to smash him to a pulp. Or perhaps, under the familiar white apron, the disfigured hand was actually clutching a pistol.

Mr. Budd retreated to the back of the shop, collecting his materials. If only he had been quicker—more like a detective in a book—he would have observed that thumbnail, that tooth, put two and two together, and run out to give the alarm while the man's head was wet and soapy and his face buried in the towel. Or he could have dabbed lather into his eyes— nobody could possibly commit a murder or even run away down the street with his eyes full of soap.

Even now—Mr. Budd took down a bottle, shook his head, and put it back on the shelf—even now, was it really too late? Why could he not take a bold course? He had only to open a razor, go quietly up behind the unsuspecting man, and say in a firm, loud, convincing voice: "William Strickland, put up your hands. Your life is at my mercy. Stand up till I take your gun away. Now walk straight out to the nearest policeman." Surely, in his position, that was what Sherlock Holmes would do.

But as Mr. Budd returned with a little trayful of requirements, it was borne in upon him that he was not of the stuff of which great manhunters are made. For he could not seriously see that attempt "coming off." Because if he held the razor to the man's throat and said: "Put up your hands," the man would probably catch him by the wrists and take the razor away. And greatly as Mr. Budd feared his customer unarmed, he felt it would be a perfect crescendo of madness to put a razor into his hands.

Or, supposing he said, "Put up your hands," and the man just said, "I won't." What was he to do next? To cut his throat then and there would be murder, even if Mr. Budd could possibly bring himself to do such a thing. They could not remain there, fixed in one position, till the boy came to do out the shop in the morning.

Perhaps the policeman would notice the light on and the door unfastened and come in? Then he would say, "I congratulate you Mr. Budd, on having captured a very dangerous criminal." But supposing the policeman didn't happen to notice—and Mr. Budd would have to stand all the time, and he would get exhausted and his attention would relax, and then—

After all, Mr. Budd wasn't called upon to arrest the man himself. "Information leading to arrest"—those were the words. He would be able to tell them the wanted man had been there, that he would now have dark brown hair and mustache and no beard. He might even shadow him when he left—he might—

It was at this moment that the great Inspiration came to Mr. Budd.

As he fetched a bottle from the glass-fronted case he remembered, with odd vividness, an old-fashioned wooden paper-knife that had belonged to his mother. Between springs of blue forget-me-not, hand-painted, it bore the inscription "Knowledge is Power."

A strange freedom and confidence were vouchsafed to Mr. Budd; his mind was alert; he removed the razors with an easy, natural movement, and made nonchalant conversation as he skillfully applied the dark-brown tint.

The streets were less crowded when Mr. Budd let his customer out. He watched the tall figure cross Grosvenor Place and climb on to a 24 bus.

"But that was only his artfulness," said Mr. Budd, as he put on his hat and coat and extinguished the lights carefully, "he'll take another at Victoria, like as not, and be making tracks from Charing Cross or Waterloo."

He closed the shop door, shook it, as was his wont, to make sure that the lock had caught properly, and in his turn made his way, by means of a 24, to the top of Whitehall.

The policeman was a little condescending at first when Mr. Budd demanded to see "somebody very high up," but finding the little barber insist so earnestly that he had news of the Manchester murderer, and that there wasn't any time to lose, he consented to pass him through.

Mr. Budd was interviewed first by an important-looking inspector in uniform, who listened very politely to his story and made him repeat very carefully about the gold tooth and the thumbnail and the hair which had been black before it was gray or red and was now dark brown.

The inspector touched a bell, and said, "Perkins, I think Sir Andrew would like to see this gentleman at once," and he was taken to another room, where sat a very shrewd, genial gentleman in mufti, who heard him with even greater attention, and called in another inspector to listen too, and to take down a very exact description of the—yes, surely the undoubted William Strickland as he now appeared.

"But there's one thing more," said Mr. Budd—"and I'm sure to goodness," he added, "I hope, sir, it is the right man, because if it isn't it'll be the ruin of me—"

He crushed his soft hat into an agitated ball as he leaned across the table, breathlessly uttering the story of his great professional betrayal.

"Tzee–z-z-z–tzee–tzee–z-z–tzee–z-z—"
    "Dzoo–dz-dz-dz–dzoo–dz–dzoo–dzoo–dz—"
    "Tzee–z-z."

The fingers of the wireless operator on the packet *Miranda* bound for Ostend moved swiftly as they jotted down the messages of the buzzing wireless mosquito swarms.

One of them made him laugh.

"The Old Man'd better have this, I suppose," he said.

The Old Man scratched his head when he read and rang a little bell for the steward. The steward ran down to the little round office where the purser was counting out his money and checking it before he locked it away for the night. On receiving the Old Man's message, the purser put the money quickly into the safe, picked up the passenger list, and departed aft. There was a short consultation, and the bell was rung again—this time to summon the head steward.

"Tzee–z-z–tzee–z-z-z–tzee–tzee–z–tzee."

All down the Channel, all over the North Sea, up to the Mersey Docks, out into the Atlantic soared the busy mosquito swarms. In ship after ship the wireless operator sent his message to the captain, the captain sent for the purser, the purser sent for the head steward, and the head steward called his staff about him. Huge liners, little packets, destroyers, sumptuous private yachts—every floating thing that carried aerials—every port in England, France, Holland, Germany, Denmark, Norway, every police center that could interpret the mosquito message, heard, between laughter and excitement, the tale of Mr. Budd's betrayal. Two Boy Scouts at Croydon, practicing their Morse with a homemade valve set, decoded it laboriously into an exercise book.

"Cripes," said Jim to George, "what a joke! D'you think they'll get the beggar?"

The *Miranda* docked at Ostend at 7 A.M. A man burst hurriedly into the cabin where the wireless operator was just taking off his headphones.

"Here!" he cried; "this is to go. There's something up and the Old Man's sent over for the police. The Consul's coming on board."

The wireless operator groaned, and switched on his valves.

"Tzee–z–tzee—" a message to the English police.

"Man on board answering to description. Ticket booked name of Watson. Has locked himself in cabin and refuses to come out. Insists on having hairdresser sent out to him. Have communicated Ostend police. Await instructions."

The Old Man with sharp words and authoritative gestures cleared a way through the excited little knot of people gathered about First Class Cabin No. 36. Several passengers had got wind of "something up." Magnificently he herded them away to the gangway with their bags and suitcases. Sternly he bade the stewards and the boy, who stood gaping with his hands full of breakfast dishes, to stand away from the door. Terribly he commanded them to hold their tongues. Four or five sailors stood watchfully at his side. In the restored silence, the passenger in No. 36 could be heard pacing up and down the narrow cabin, moving things, clattering, splashing water.

Presently came steps overhead. Somebody arrived, with a

message. The Old Man nodded. Six pairs of Belgian police boots came tiptoeing down the companion. The Old Man glanced at the official paper held out to him and nodded again.

"Ready?"

"Yes."

The Old Man knocked at the door of No. 36.

"Who is it?" cried a harsh, sharp voice.

"The barber is here, sir, that you sent for."

"Ah!" There was relief in the tone. "Send him in alone, if you please. I—I have had an accident."

"Yes, sir."

At the sound of the bolt being cautiously withdrawn, the Old Man stepped forward. The door opened a chink, and was slammed to again, but the Old Man's boot was firmly wedged against the jamb. The policemen surged forward. There was a yelp and a shot which smashed harmlessly through the window of the first-class saloon, and the passenger was brought out.

"Strike me pink!" shrieked the boy, "strike me pink if he ain't gone green in the night!"

Not for nothing had Mr. Budd studied the intricate mutual reactions of chemical dyes. In the pride of his knowledge he had set a mark on his man, to mark him out from all the billions of this overpopulated world. Was there a port in all Christendom where a murderer might slip away, with every hair on him green as a parrot—green mustache, green eyebrows, and that thick, springing shock of hair, vivid, flaring midsummer green?

Mr Budd got his £500. The *Evening Messenger* published the full story of his great betrayal. He trembled, fearing this sinister fame. Surely no one would ever come to him again.

On the next morning an enormous blue limousine rolled up to his door, to the immense admiration of Wilton Street. A lady, magnificent in muskrat and diamonds, swept into the little saloon.

"You *are* Mr. Budd, aren't you?" she cried. "The *great* Mr. Budd? Isn't it *too* wonderful? And now, dear Mr. Budd, you *must* do me a favor. You must dye my hair green, *at once. Now.* I want to be able to say I'm the *very first* to be done by *you.* I'm the Duchess of Winchester, and that awful Melcaster woman is chasing me down the street—the cat!"

If you want it done, I can give you the number of Mr. Budd's parlors in Bond Street. But I understand it is a terribly expensive process.

FROM THE FILES OF INSPECTOR CRAIG

RAYMOND SMULLYAN

Part of the pleasure we get from detective stories is the sheer puzzle element. Given certain clues and using only logic, what can we definitely deduce? These puzzles in logic were written by a professor of mathematical logic who has also performed as a professional magician. If anyone should know about puzzling, he should. All the clues you need to solve them are right there in the open. How many can you work out?

INSPECTOR LESLIE CRAIG of Scotland Yard has kindly consented to release some of his case histories for the benefit of those interested in the application of logic to the solution of crimes.

1

We shall start with a simple case. An enormous amount of loot had been stolen from a store. The criminal (or criminals) took the heist away in a car. Three well-known criminals A, B, C were brought to Scotland Yard for questioning. The following facts were ascertained:

(1) No one other than A, B, C was involved in the robbery.

(2) C never pulls a job without using A (and possibly others) as an accomplice.

(3) B does not know how to drive.

Is A innocent or guilty?

2

Another simple case, again of robbery. A, B, C were brought in for questioning and the following facts were ascertained:

(1) No one other than A, B, C was involved.

(2) A never works without at least one accomplice.

(3) C is innocent.

Is B innocent or guilty?

3

In this more interesting case, the robbery occurred in London. Three well-known criminals A, B, C were rounded up for questioning. Now, A and C happened to be identical twins and few people could tell them apart. All three suspects had elaborate records, and a good deal was known about their personalities and habits. In particular, the twins were quite timid, and neither one ever dared to pull a job without an accomplice. B, on the other hand, was quite bold and despised ever using an accomplice. Also several witnesses testified that at the time of the robbery, one of the two twins was seen drinking at a bar in Dover, but it was not known which twin.

Again, assuming that no one other than A, B, C was involved in the robbery, which ones are innocent and which ones guilty?

For Inspector Craig's solutions see page 221.

BUTCH MINDS THE BABY

DAMON RUNYON

Damon Runyon began his writing career as a journalist specializing in sports. He soon turned to writing short stories about the gamblers, drinkers, night-club dancers, and minor crooks who spent their time on New York's Broadway making bets, striking deals, and generally getting up to no good, but having a wonderful time doing it. Strictly speaking, they aren't exactly detective stories, but this one was too much fun to leave out.

He used a lot of slang, and his style is a distinctive part of his storytelling. This is a story about three of his favorite characters and their attempt to persuade a safe-breaker to join them in a burglary.

The trouble is, he's promised his wife to look after the baby . . .

O NE EVENING along about seven o'clock I am sitting in Mindy's restaurant putting on the gefillte fish, which is a dish I am very fond of, when in comes three parties from Brooklyn wearing caps as follows: Harry the Horse, Little Isadore, and Spanish John.

Now these parties are not such parties as I will care to have much truck with, because I often hear rumors about them that are very discreditable, even if the rumors are not true. In fact, I hear that many citizens of Brooklyn will be very glad indeed to see Harry the Horse, Little Isadore, and Spanish

John move away from there, as they are always doing something that is considered a knock to the community, such as robbing people, or maybe shooting or stabbing them, and throwing pineapples, and carrying on generally.

I am really much surprised to see these parties on Broadway, as it is well known that the Broadway coppers just naturally love to shove such parties around, but here they are in Mindy's, and there I am, so of course I give them a very large hello, as I never wish to seem inhospitable, even to Brooklyn parties. Right away they come over to my table and sit down, and Little Isadore reaches out and spears himself a big hunk of my gefillte fish with his fingers, but I overlook this, as I am using the only knife on the table.

Then they all sit there looking at me without saying anything, and the way they look at me makes me very nervous indeed. Finally I figure that maybe they are a little embarrassed being in a high-class spot such as Mindy's, with legitimate people around and about, so I say to them, very polite:

"It is a nice night."

"What is nice about it?" asks Harry the Horse, who is a thin man with a sharp face and sharp eyes.

Well, now that it is put up to me in this way, I can see there is nothing so nice about the night, at that, so I try to think of something else jolly to say, while Little Isadore keeps spearing at my gefillte ish with his fing , and Spanish John nabs one of my potatoes.

"Where does Big Butch live?" Harry the Horse asks.

"Big Butch?" I say, as if I never hear the name before in my life, because in this man's town it is never a good idea to answer any question without thinking it over, as some time you may give the wrong answer to the wrong guy, or the wrong answer to the right guy. "Where does Big Butch live?" I ask them again.

"Yes, where does he live?" Harry the Horse says, very impatient. "We wish you to take us to him."

"Now wait a minute, Harry," I say, and I am now more

nervous than somewhat. "I am not sure I remember the exact house Big Butch lives in, and furthermore I am not sure Big Butch will care to have me bringing people to see him, especially three at a time, and especially from Brooklyn. You know Big Butch has a very bad disposition, and there is no telling what he may say to me if he does not like the idea of me taking you to him."

"Everything is very kosher," Harry the Horse says. "You need not be afraid of anything whatever. We have a business proposition for Big Butch. It means a nice score for him, so you take us to him at once, or the chances are I will have to put the arm on somebody around here."

Well, as the only one around there for him to put the arm on at this time seems to be me, I can see where it will be good policy for me to take these parties to Big Butch, especially as the last of my gefillte fish is just going down Little Isadore's gullet, and Spanish John is finishing up my potatoes, and is donking a piece of rye bread in my coffee, so there is nothing for me to eat.

So I lead them over into West Forty-ninth Street, near Tenth Avenue, where Big Butch lives on the ground floor of an old brownstone-front house, and who is sitting out on the stoop but Big Butch himself. In fact, everybody in the neighborhood is sitting out on the front stoops over there, including women and children, because sitting out on the front stoops is quite a custom in this section.

Big Butch is peeled down to his undershirt and pants, and he has no shoes on his feet, as Big Butch is a guy who likes his comfort. Furthermore, he is smoking a cigar, and laid out on the stoop beside him on a blanket is a little baby with not much clothes on. This baby seems to be asleep, and every now and then Big Butch fans it with a folded newspaper to shoo away the mosquitoes that wish to nibble on the baby. These mosquitoes come across the river from the Jersey side on hot nights and they seem to be very fond of babies.

"Hello, Butch," I say, as we stop in front of the stoop.

"Sh-h-h-h!" Butch says, pointing at the baby, and making

more noise with his shush than an engine blowing off steam. Then he gets up and tiptoes down to the sidewalk where we are standing, and I am hoping that Butch feels all right, because when Butch does not feel so good he is apt to be very short with one and all. He is a guy of maybe six foot two and a couple of feet wide, and he has big hairy hands and a mean look.

In fact, Big Butch is known all over this man's town as a guy you must not monkey with in any respect, so it takes plenty of weight off of me when I see that he seems to know the parties from Brooklyn, and nods at them very friendly, especially at Harry the Horse. And right away Harry states a most surprising proposition to Big Butch.

It seems that there is a big coal company which has an office in an old building down in West Eighteenth Street, and in this office is a safe, and in this safe is the company payroll of twenty thousand dollars cash money. Harry the Horse knows the money is there because a personal friend of his who is the paymaster for the company puts it there late this very afternoon.

It seems that the paymaster enters into a dicker with Harry the Horse and Little Isadore and Spanish John for them to slug him while he is carrying the payroll from the bank to the office in the afternoon, but something happens that they miss connections on the exact spot, so the paymaster has to carry the sugar on to the office without being slugged, and there it is now in two fat bundles.

Personally it seems to me as I listen to Harry's story that the paymaster must be a very dishonest character to be making deals to hold still while he is being slugged and the company's sugar taken away from him, but of course it is none of my business, so I take no part in the conversation.

Well, it seems Harry the Horse and Little Isadore and Spanish John wish to get the money out of the safe, but none of them knows anything about opening safes, and while they are standing around over in Brooklyn talking over what is to be done in this emergency Harry suddenly remembers that

99

Big Butch is once in the business of opening safes for a living.

In fact, I hear afterwards that Big Butch is considered the best safe opener east of the Mississippi River in his day, but the law finally takes to sending him to Sing Sing for opening these safes, and after he is in and out of Sing Sing three different times for opening safes Butch gets sick and tired of the place, especially as they pass what is called Baumes Law in New York, which is a law that says if a guy is sent to Sing Sing four times hand running, he must stay there the rest of his life, without any argument about it.

So Big Butch gives up opening safes for a living, and goes into business in a small way, such as running beer, and handling a little Scotch now and then, and becomes an honest citizen. Furthermore, he marries one of his neighbor's children over on the West Side by the name of Mary Murphy, and I judge the baby on this stoop comes of this marriage between Big Butch and Mary because I can see that it is a very homely baby, indeed. Still, I never see many babies that I consider rose geraniums for looks, anyway.

Well, it finally comes out that the idea of Harry the Horse and Little Isadore and Spanish John is to get Big Butch to open the coal company's safe and take the payroll money out, and they are willing to give him fifty percent of the money for his bother, taking fifty percent for themselves for finding the plant, and paying all the overhead, such as the paymaster, out of their bit, which strikes me as a pretty fair sort of deal for Big Butch. But Butch only shakes his head.

"It is old-fashioned stuff," Butch says. "Nobody opens pete boxes for a living anymore. They make the boxes too good, and they are all wired up with alarms and are a lot of trouble generally. I am in a legitimate business now and going along. You boys know I cannot stand another fall, what with being away three times already, and in addition to this I must mind the baby. My old lady goes to Mrs. Clancy's wake tonight up in the Bronx, and the chances are she will be there all night, as she is very fond of wakes, so I must mind little John Ignatius Junior."

"Listen, Butch," Harry the Horse says, "this is a very soft pete. It is old-fashioned, and you can open it with a toothpick. There are no wires on it, because they never put more than a dime in it before in years. It just happens they have to put the twenty G's in it tonight because my pal the paymaster makes it a point not to get back from the jug with the scratch in time to pay off today, especially after he sees we miss out on him. It is the softest touch you will ever know, and where can a guy pick up ten G's like this?"

I can see that Big Butch is thinking the ten G's over very seriously, at that, because in these times nobody can afford to pass up ten G's, especially a guy in the beer business, which is very, very tough just now. But finally he shakes his head again and says like this:

"No," he says, "I must let it go, because I must mind the baby. My old lady is very, very particular about this, and I dast not leave little John Ignatius Junior for a minute. If Mary comes home and finds I am not minding the baby she will put the blast on me plenty. I like to turn a few honest bobs now and then as well as anybody, but," Butch says, "John Ignatius Junior comes first with me."

Then he turns away and goes back to the stoop as much as to say he is through arguing, and sits down beside John Ignatius Junior again just in time to keep a mosquito from carrying off one of John's legs. Anybody can see that Big Butch is very fond of this baby, though personally I will not give you a dime a dozen for babies, male and female.

Well, Harry the Horse and Little Isadore and Spanish John are very much disappointed, and stand around talking among themselves, and paying no attention to me, when all of a sudden Spanish John, who never has much to say up to this time, seems to have a bright idea. He talks to Harry and Isadore, and they get all pleasured up over what he has to say, and finally Harry goes to Big Butch.

"Sh-h-h-h!" Big Butch says, pointing to the baby as Harry opens his mouth.

"Listen, Butch," Harry says in a whisper, "we can take the

101

baby with us, and you can mind it and work, too."

"Why," Big Butch whispers back, "this is quite an idea indeed. Let us go into the house and talk things over."

So he picks up the baby and leads us into his joint, and gets out some pretty fair beer, though it is needled a little, at that, and we sit around the kitchen chewing the fat in whispers. There is a crib in the kitchen, and Butch puts the baby in this crib, and it keeps on snoozing away first rate while we are talking. In fact, it is sleeping so sound that I am commencing to figure that Butch must give it some of the needled beer he is feeding us, because I am feeling a little dopey myself.

Finally Butch says that as long as he can take John Ignatius Junior with him he sees no reason why he shall not go and open the safe for them, only he says he must have five percent more to put in the baby's bank when he gets back, so as to round himself up with his ever-loving wife in case of a beef from her over keeping the baby out in the night air. Harry the Horse says he considers this extra five percent a little strong, but Spanish John, who seems to be a very square guy, says that after all it is only fair to cut the baby in if it is to be with them when they are making the score, and Little Isadore seems to think this is all right, too. So Harry the Horse gives in, and says five percent it is.

Well, as they do not wish to start out until after midnight, and as there is plenty of time, Big Butch gets out some more needled beer, and then he goes looking for the tools with which he opens safes, and which he says he does not see since the day John Ignatius Junior is born and he gets them out to build the crib.

Now this is a good time for me to bid one and all farewell, and what keeps me there is something I cannot tell you to this day, because personally I never before have any idea of taking part in a safe opening, especially with a baby, as I consider such actions very dishonorable. When I come to think things over afterwards, the only thing I can figure is the needled beer, but I wish to say I am really very much surprised at myself when I find myself in a taxicab along about one o'clock in the morning with these Brooklyn parties and Big Butch and the baby.

Butch has John Ignatius Junior rolled up in a blanket, and John is still pounding his ear. Butch has a satchel of tools, and what looks to me like a big flat book, and just before we leave the house Butch hands me a package and tells me to be very careful with it. He gives Little Isadore a smaller package, which Isadore shoves into his pistol pocket, and when Isadore sits down in the taxi something goes wa-wa, like a sheep, and Big Butch becomes very indignant because it seems Isadore is sitting on John Ignatius Junior's doll, which says "Mamma" when you squeeze it.

It seems Big Butch figures that John Ignatius Junior may wish something to play with in case he wakes up, and it is a good thing for Little Isadore that the mamma doll is not squashed so it cannot say "Mamma" anymore, or the chances are Little Isadore will get a good bust in the snoot.

We let the taxicab go a block away from the spot we are headed for in West Eighteenth Street, between Seventh and Eighth Avenues, and walk the rest of the way two by two. I walk with Big Butch, carrying my package, and Butch is lugging the baby and his satchel and the flat thing that looks like a book. It is so quiet down in West Eighteenth Street at such an hour that you can hear yourself think, and in fact I hear myself thinking very plain that I am a big sap to be on a job like this, especially with a baby, but I keep going just the same, which shows you what a very big sap I am, indeed.

There are very few people in West Eighteenth Street when we get there, and one of them is a fat guy who is leaning against a building almost in the center of the block, and who takes a walk for himself as soon as he sees us. It seems that this fat guy is the watchman at the coal company's office and is also a personal friend of Harry the Horse, which is why he takes the walk when he sees us coming.

It is agreed before we leave Big Butch's house that Harry the Horse and Spanish John are to stay outside the place as lookouts, while Big Butch is inside opening the safe, and that

Little Isadore is to go with Butch. Nothing whatever is said by anybody about where I am to be at any time, and I can see that, no matter where I am, I will still be an outsider, but, as Butch gives me the package to carry, I figure he wishes me to remain with him.

It is no bother at all getting into the office of the coal company, which is on the ground floor, because it seems the watchman leaves the door open, this watchman being a most obliging guy, indeed. In fact he is so obliging that by and by he comes back and lets Harry the Horse and Spanish John tie him up good and tight, and stick a handkerchief in his mouth and chuck him in an areaway next to the office, so nobody will think he has anything to do with opening the safe in case anybody comes around asking.

The office looks out on the street, and the safe that Harry the Horse and Little Isadore and Spanish John wish Big Butch to open is standing up against the rear wall of the office facing the street windows. There is one little electric light burning very dim over the safe so that when anybody walks past the place outside, such as a watchman, they can look through the window and see the safe at all times, unless they are blind. It is not a tall safe, and it is not a big safe, and I can see Big Butch grin when he sees it, so I figure this safe is not much of a safe, just as Harry the Horse claims.

Well, as soon as Big Butch and the baby and Little Isadore and me get into the office, Big Butch steps over to the safe and unfolds what I think is the big flat book, and what is it but a sort of screen painted on one side to look exactly like the front of a safe. Big Butch stands this screen up on the floor in front of the real safe, leaving plenty of space in between, the idea being that the screen will keep anyone passing in the street outside from seeing Butch while he is opening the safe, because when a man is opening a safe he needs all the privacy he can get.

Big Butch lays John Ignatius Junior down on the floor on the blanket behind the phony safe front and takes his tools out of the satchel and starts to work opening the safe, while

Little Isadore and me get back in a corner where it is dark, because there is not room for all of us back of the screen. However, we can see what Big Butch is doing, and I wish to say while I never before see a professional safe opener at work, and never wish to see another, this Butch handles himself like a real artist.

He starts drilling into the safe around the combination lock, working very fast and very quiet, when all of a sudden what happens but John Ignatius Junior sits up on the blanket and lets out a squall. Naturally this is most disquieting to me, and personally I am in favor of beaning John Ignatius Junior with something to keep him still, because I am nervous enough as it is. But the squalling does not seem to bother Big Butch. He lays down his tools and picks up John Ignatius Junior and starts whispering, "There, there, there, my itty oddleums. Da-dad is here."

Well, this sounds very nonsensical to me in such a situation, and it makes no impression whatever on John Ignatius Junior. He keeps on squalling, and I judge he is squalling pretty loud because I see Harry the Horse and Spanish John both walk past the window and look in very anxious. Big Butch jiggles John Ignatius Junior up and down and keeps whispering baby talk to him, which sounds very undignified coming from a high-class safe opener, and finally Butch whispers to me to hand him the package I am carrying.

He opens the package, and what is in it but a baby's nursing bottle full of milk. Moreover, there is a little tin stew pan, and Butch hands the pan to me and whispers to me to find a water tap somewhere in the joint and fill the pan with water. So I go stumbling around in the dark in a room behind the office and bark my shins several times before I find a tap and fill the pan. I take it back to Big Butch, and he squats there with the baby on one arm, and gets a tin of what is called canned heat out of the package, and lights this canned heat with his cigar lighter, and starts heating the pan of water with the nursing bottle in it.

Big Butch keeps sticking his finger in the pan of water while it is heating, and by and by he puts the rubber nipple of the nursing bottle in his mouth and takes a pull at it to see if the milk is warm enough, just like I see dolls who have babies do. Apparently the milk is okay, as Butch hands the bottle to John Ignatius Junior, who grabs hold of it with both hands and starts sucking on the business end. Naturally he has to stop squalling, and Big Butch goes to work on the safe again, with John Ignatius Junior sitting on the blanket, pulling on the bottle and looking wiser than a treeful of owls.

It seems the safe is either a tougher job than anybody figures, or Big Butch's tools are not so good, what with being old and rusty and used for building baby cribs, because he breaks a couple of drills and works himself up into quite a sweat without getting anywhere. Butch afterwards explains to me that he is one of the first guys in this country to open safes without explosives, but he says to do this work properly you have to know the safes so as to drill to the tumblers of the lock just right, and it seems that this particular safe is a new type to him, even if it is old, and he is out of practice.

Well, in the meantime John Ignatius Junior finishes his bottle and starts mumbling again, and Big Butch gives him a tool to play with, and finally Butch needs this tool and tries to take it away from John Ignatius Junior, and the baby lets out such a squawk that Butch has to let him keep it until he can sneak it away from him, and this causes more delay.

Finally Big Butch gives up trying to drill the safe open, and he whispers to us that he will have to put a little shot in it to loosen up the lock, which is all right with us, because we are getting tired of hanging around and listening to John Ignatius Junior's glug-glugging. As far as I am personally concerned, I am wishing I am home in bed.

Well, Butch starts pawing through his satchel looking for something and it seems that what he is looking for is a little bottle of some kind of explosive with which to shake the lock on the safe up some, and at first he cannot find this bottle, but finally he discovers that John Ignatius Junior has it and is gnawing at the cork, and Butch has quite a battle making John Ignatius Junior give it up.

Anyway, he fixes the explosive in one of the holes he drills near the combination lock on the safe, and then he puts in a fuse, and just before he touches off the fuse Butch picks up John Ignatius Junior and hands him to Little Isadore, and tells us to go into the room behind the office. John Ignatius Junior does not seem to care for Little Isadore, and I do not blame him, at that, because he starts to squirm around quite some in Isadore's arms and lets out a squall, but all of a sudden he becomes very quiet indeed, and, while I am not able to prove it, something tells me that Little Isadore has his hand over John Ignatius Junior's mouth.

Well, Big Butch joins us right away in the back room, and sound comes out of John Ignatius Junior again as Butch takes him from Little Isadore, and I am thinking that it is a good thing for Isadore that the baby cannot tell Big Butch what Isadore does to him.

"I put in just a little bit of shot," Big Butch says, "and it will not make any more noise than snapping your fingers."

But a second later there is a big whoom from the office, and the whole joint shakes, and John Ignatius Junior laughs right out loud. The chances are he thinks it is the Fourth of July.

"I guess maybe I put in too big a charge," Big Butch says, and then he rushes into the office with Little Isadore and me after him, and John Ignatius Junior still laughing very heartily for a small baby. The door of the safe is swinging loose, and the whole joint looks somewhat wrecked, but Big Butch loses no time in getting his dukes into the safe and grabbing out two big bundles of cash money, which he sticks inside his shirt.

As we go into the street Harry the Horse and Spanish John come running up much excited, and Harry says to Big Butch like this:

"What are you trying to do," he says, "wake up the whole town?"

"Well," Butch says, "I guess maybe the charge is too strong, at that, but nobody seems to be coming, so you and Spanish John walk over to Eighth Avenue, and the rest of us will walk to Seventh, and if you go along quiet, like people minding their own business, it will be all right."

But I judge Little Isadore is tired of John Ignatius Junior's company by this time, because he says he will go with Harry the Horse and Spanish John, and this leaves Big Butch and John Ignatius Junior and me to go the other way. So we start moving, and all of a sudden two cops come tearing around the corner toward which Harry and Isadore and Spanish John are going. The chances are the cops hear the earthquake Big Butch lets off and are coming to investigate.

But the chances are, too, that if Harry the Horse and the other two keep on walking along very quietly like Butch tells them to, the coppers will pass them up entirely, because it is not likely that coppers will figure anybody to be opening safes with explosives in this neighborhood. But the minute Harry the Horse sees the coppers he loses his nut, and he outs with the old equalizer and starts blasting away, and what does Spanish John do but get his out, too, and open up.

The next thing anybody knows, the two coppers are down on the ground with slugs in them, but other coppers are coming from every which direction, blowing whistles and doing a little blasting themselves, and there is plenty of excitement, especially when the coppers who are not chasing Harry the Horse and Little Isadore and Spanish John start poking around the neighborhood and find Harry's pal, the watchman, all tied up nice and tight where Harry leaves him, and the watchman explains that some scoundrels blow open the safe he is watching.

All this time Big Butch and me are walking in the other direction toward Seventh Avenue, and Big Butch has John Ignatius in his arms, and John Ignatius is now squalling very loud, indeed. The chances are he is still thinking of the big whoom back there which tickles him so and is wishing to hear some more whooms. Anyway, he is beating his own best record for squalling, and as we go walking along Big Butch say to me like this:

"I dast not run," he says, "because if any coppers see me running they will start popping at me and maybe hit John

Ignatius Junior, and besides running will joggle the milk up in him and make him sick. My old lady always warns me never to joggle John Ignatius Junior when he is full of milk."

"Well, Butch," I say, "there is no milk in me, and I do not care if I am joggled up, so if you do not mind, I will start doing a piece of running at the next corner."

But just then around the corner of Seventh Avenue toward which we are headed comes two or three coppers with a big fat sergeant with them, and one of the coppers, who is half out of breath as if he has been doing plenty of sprinting, is explaining to the sergeant that somebody blows a safe down the street and shoots a couple of coppers in the getaway.

And there is Big Butch, with John Ignatius Junior in his arms and twenty G's in his shirt front and a tough record behind him, walking right up to them.

I am feeling very sorry, indeed, for Big Butch, and very sorry for myself, too, and I am saying to myself that if I get out of this I will never associate with anyone but ministers of the gospel as long as I live. I can remember thinking that I am getting a better break than Butch, at that, because I will not have to go to Sing Sing for the rest of my life, like him, and I also remember wondering what they will give John Ignatius Junior, who is still tearing off these squalls, with Big Butch saying, "There, there, there, Daddy's itty woggleums." Then I hear one of the coppers say to the fat sergeant:

"We better nail these guys. They may be in on this."

Well, I can see it is goodbye to Butch and John Ignatius Junior and me, as the fat sergeant steps up to Big Butch, but instead of putting the arm on Butch, the fat sergeant only points at John Ignatius Junior and asks very sympathetic:

"Teeth?"

"No," Big Butch says. "Not teeth. Colic. I just get the doctor here out of bed to do something for him, and we are going to a drugstore to get some medicine."

Well, naturally I am very much surprised at this statement, because of course I am not a doctor, and if John Ignatius Junior has colic it serves him right, but I am only hoping they do not ask for my degree, when the fat sergeant says:

"Too bad. I know what it is. I got three of them at home. But," he says, "it acts more like it is teeth than colic."

Then as Big Butch and John Ignatius Junior and me go on about our business I hear the fat sergeant say to the copper, very sarcastic:

"Yea, of course a guy is out blowing safes with a baby in his arms! You will make a great detective, you will!"

I do not see Big Butch for several days after I learn that Harry the Horse and Little Isadore and Spanish John get back to Brooklyn all right, except they are a little nicked up here and there from the slugs the coppers toss at them, while the coppers they clip are not damaged so very much. Furthermore, the chances are I will not see Big Butch for several years, if it is left to me, but he comes looking for me one night, and he seems to be all pleasured up about something.

"Say," Big Butch says to me, "you know I never give a copper credit for knowing any too much about anything, but I wish to say that this fat sergeant we run into the other night is a very, very smart duck. He is right about it being teeth that is ailing John Ignatius Junior, for what happens yesterday but John cuts his first tooth."

MURDER AT ST. OSWALD'S

MICHAEL UNDERWOOD

A closed community, like the old-fashioned boarding school in which this story is set, is a very good place to set a detective story. All the suspects are close at hand; tensions can build up quickly; suspicions can fall on the most unlikely people . . .

And even when a planned murder goes wrong, there might still be a body in the shed.

"I THINK HE SHOULD be sentenced to be boiled in oil," said Wace, who was aged eleven.

His friend, Webster, nodded enthusiastically. "Yes, then be thrown into a pit full of poisonous spiders and scorpions."

Nigel Kilby frowned impatiently. He was the recognized leader of their form and the acknowledged foreman of their self-constituted jury, for it so happened that middle school (the name of their form) had exactly twelve pupils.

"That's silly," he said scathingly. "Where'd you get enough oil?"

"And where would you find poisonous spiders and scorpions?" inquired Marsden, the form's best all-rounder.

"I'd steal them from a zoo," Webster said robustly.

"And I'd get oil from a garage," added Wace, "and heat it in a cauldron."

112

Nigel Kilby was still frowning. "We've got to think of some terribly clever way of killing him," he said. "Something that can never be detected."

"I was reading in a magazine about a tribe in some jungle who kill their enemies with poison darts. They use blowpipes and the poison is so deadly that the person dies immediately." This contribution came from Perry mi who was the smallest and, at ten, the youngest boy in the form.

Kilby nodded. "Poison is definitely the best way."

"We could push him over the cliff on a walk," Marsden said. "We'd say it was an accident, that he went too close to the edge and it crumbled."

"That'd be all right if we could be certain it'd kill him," Kilby conceded. "But supposing he was only injured. Supposing he managed to hang on to something . . ."

A silence fell as each of them contemplated the full horror of such a plan going awry. The existing tyranny would be nothing compared with what would inevitably follow.

There was no doubt that Mr. Cheeseman was the most unpopular master at St. Oswald's, and the boys of middle school, of which he was the form master, were further convinced that he must be the most hated master in any of the preparatory schools strung out along the Sussex coast in that year of 1929. Whenever they compared notes with boys from neighboring schools, it served to confirm their morbid conviction that "Cheesepot" was Attila the Hun, Ghengis Khan, and Fouquier-Tinville rolled into one. They accepted from Kilby that you couldn't find a nastier trio in history.

Mr. Cheeseman—Cheesepot behind his back—was a tall, lean man with a heavy mustache and a deep voice which could sound more threatening than any roll of thunder. He had drifted into teaching after coming out of the army in 1919 and had been at St. Oswald's for six years. Like many of his sort at the time, he had no academic qualifications, merely a basic knowledge of the subjects he taught, and an ability to maintain discipline and lend a crude hand at games. Even allowing for the boys' natural exaggeration, a dispassionate adult eye could not have failed to notice that he took a distinct relish in tormenting his pupils. He was not only a bully, he was also unfair. For example, just recently he had kept Webster behind and made him late for prayers and had then told the headmaster there was no reason why Webster should not have been there on time. When Webster had made a muted protest, Mr. Cheeseman had given a nasty sort of laugh and said, "Life is unfair, boy. The sooner you realize it, the better."

"I bet Mrs. Cheeseman'll be glad when he dies," Wace said, breaking the silence that had fallen.

The Cheesemans lived in a cottage on the edge of the school grounds and Mrs. Cheeseman helped matron with the boys' clothes. She was a small, pale, soft-spoken woman, who appeared to be as much dominated by her husband as were the boys of his form. She aroused their sense of chivalry and they had little doubt that she would welcome her husband's demise as much as they would.

"I bet he pulls her hair," Webster added.

"How are we going to poison him, Kilby?" Marsden asked, getting the discussion back on course again.

"What we need," Kilby said slowly to his now attentive audience, "is a poison that'll take a bit of time to work. I mean, we can mix it with his porridge at breakfast, but we don't want him to drop dead until later, so that no one will guess when he took it."

"Like when he's in the shed mending the mower," Marsden remarked.

One of Mr. Cheeseman's responsibilities was looking after the school's large motor mower. He appeared to have a far greater affinity for its oily workings than he did for his pupils and he was forever tinkering with its engine.

"But where'll you get the poison, Kilby?" Wace asked.

"I'll have to look in my book. It'll probably mean making our own poison. There are all sorts of poisonous things in the school wood."

"It'd have to be tasteless," Marsden observed.

114

"That's not difficult," Kilby said confidently. "And, anyway, the porridge is so revolting, no one could tell whether it'd been poisoned or not."

Perry mi gave a sudden, frightened start and bent studiously over his desk. One or two boys turned their heads and then quickly followed suit, for standing in the doorway with a disagreeable gleam in his eye was Mr. Cheeseman. How long he had been there and what, if anything, he had overheard they were not to know, but a chilly fear gripped each of them.

They sat in two rows of six and it was Mr. Cheeseman himself who had sardonically likened them unto a jury. They now gazed at him with expressions of anxious innocence as he mounted the small dais and faced them across the top of his desk.

The silence which followed became quickly oppressive, so that Wace felt compelled to break it.

"Good morning, sir," he said.

Mr. Cheeseman now focused his attention on Wace. His mustache twitched.

"Is it, Wace?"

Wace was nonplussed and gave a nervous giggle.

"What's the joke, Wace? Come on, share it, don't keep it to yourself," the deep voice boomed.

"Joke, sir? There isn't any joke, sir."

"But you giggled, Wace. There must be a joke. Or are you so feather-brained that you giggle at nothing?"

"I didn't know I did giggle, sir," Wace said in a tone of alarm, endeavoring to extricate himself from a rapidly deteriorating situation.

"I didn't hear him giggle, sir," Webster said loyally.

"Webster and Wace, our twin buffoons," Mr. Cheeseman observed, glancing at the faces turned toward him. Then in his most sepulchral tone he added, "But buffoonery can be a dangerous sport, so take warning!"

He picked up the top exercise book from the pile he had brought into the classroom with him. It was their French composition of the previous afternoon which he had corrected.

"Brook?"

"Here, sir."

"Evans?"

"Here, sir."

"Perry mi?"

"Here, sir."

As each boy answered to his name, his exercise book was skimmed at him like a quoit. Anyone failing to catch was made to stand with the book balanced on his head.

"Everyone got their books?" Mr. Cheeseman asked in a doom-laden tone.

"No, sir, you haven't given me mine," Wace said nervously.

"Nor I have, Wace. I've kept yours back for special presentation. Just step up here, will you?"

Wace rose and made his way slowly around the end of the desks, an expression of apprehension on his face. He paused when he reached the edge of the dais.

"Stand here, Wace," Mr. Cheeseman said, pointing at the floor beside his desk, "and face the rest of the class."

Mr. Cheeseman rose and stepped across to stand behind him. In one hand he held the exercise book; his other hand seized the hair in the nape of Wace's neck.

"What gender is *maison*, Wace?"

"Er . . . feminine, sir."

"Then why did you put *le maison*?" he barked, giving the hair a vicious tweak.

"Ouch!"

"And what is the plural of *hibou*?"

"I can't think sir, you're hurting, sir."

There was another tweak followed by a further cry of pain.

"Come on, Wace, the plural of *hibou*?"

"*H-I-B-O-U-S*."

This time there was a shriek as Mr. Cheeseman jerked his head back.

"*H-I-B-O-U-X*, you ignorant boy! There are more mistakes

in your composition, than there are pips in a pot of raspberry jam. You're lazy, Wace, and you don't pay attention."

"I do, sir."

"Don't argue with me," Mr. Cheeseman thundered, slowly rotating the hand which held the hair.

By now Wace was scarlet and tears were tumbling down his cheeks.

"Crying doesn't cut any ice with me, Wace. You'll stay in this afternoon and copy out the first ten pages of your French Grammar. Later I shall come and hear you and there'd better not be any mistakes. Now get back to your desk!" As he spoke he slapped him across the top of his head with the exercise book and then flung it after him.

A grim silence ensued in which only Wace's strangulated sobs could be heard. Webster tried to comfort his friend by picking up the book for him and helping him look for his pen which had rolled off the desk.

The rest of the lesson was passed in a more oppressive atmosphere than ever and it was not until the school bell had been rung to signal the end of the period and Mr. Cheeseman had swept out that anyone dared speak.

"Don't worry, Wace," Kilby said, "it won't be for much longer."

"Couldn't we put a spell on him?" Perry mi asked.

"What sort of spell?" Marsden inquired with interest.

"A spell to make him fall down and break both his legs."

"How do you do that?"

"I'm not really sure. But if we formed a sort of circle and held hands and closed our eyes and muttered an incantation, it might work."

"What's an incantation?" Webster asked.

"It's words for casting spells," Kilby broke in. "But I doubt if we could make it work. I still think poison's the best way. I tell you what, I'm excused games this afternoon because of my new spectacles, so I'll go into the wood and collect poisonous things. I'll look in my book first and see what would make the deadliest poison."

117

"I'll come with you," Perry mi said. "Matron's excused me games because of my cold."

Kilby nodded his approval. "We'll go off immediately after lunch while everyone's changing."

At this, even Wace managed to look more cheerful. Life without Cheesepot came as close to paradise as his imagination could bring him.

Nigel Kilby was the last to enter the classroom when they reassembled just before half-past four. He was carrying a brown cardboard box which he quickly slipped into his desk.

"What did you get?" Marsden asked.

Kilby removed the lid of the box and they all craned forward to have a look. What they saw were some mysterious pale berries, a root resembling a parsnip and a number of different leaves.

"Are they all poisonous?" Webster asked eagerly.

Kilby nodded gravely and one or two boys pulled back from the deadly contents. Yarrow even held his breath in case any fumes were being given off.

"But you can't sprinkle that lot on his porridge," Marsden remarked.

"Of course not. The poison's got to be made. The leaves have to be boiled and then the grated root and the crushed berries must be added. It's what's left at the end that's the poison." Kilby cast a quick glance toward the door before going on. "I've got a tin and I'll boil the leaves on the gas ring outside Matron's room when she's down at staff dinner tonight. But someone'll have to keep watch at the end of the corridor in case she comes back early."

"I'll do that," Marsden volunteered.

"It'll be better if Perry does it. He's smaller and can hide under the table."

"What'll the poison look like?" Wace asked.

Nigel Kilby blinked behind his spectacles. The truth was that he had no idea, but no leader could possibly make such an admission.

"It'll be a sort of nondescript powder," he said. "We'll put it on his porridge at breakfast tomorrow. You know the way he goes and talks to Mr. Saunders after serving us, I'll do it then."

"Suppose he doesn't have any porridge tomorrow?" Webster asked.

"Then we'll have to wait until the next day. But he always has porridge."

"He didn't one day last week. I remember noticing."

"That was because he'd been out drinking the night before. He's only like that on Mondays." Kilby glanced around at his eleven fellow jurors. "Don't forget we're in this together. We must take an oath of silence and swear never to tell a single soul whatever happens. If we stick together, nobody'll ever find out."

"Not even the top Scotland Yard detective," Wace added in a burst of confidence.

"So, are we all agreed, Cheesepot must die?" Kilby said, looking from face to face.

Everyone nodded, though some a trifle apprehensively.

Shortly afterward the object of their death sentence strode into the classroom. But for once he seemed preoccupied. It was supposed to be an English lesson, but all he did was to give them an essay subject and then, while they wrote, stare with a glowering expression out of the window. He didn't even shout or attempt to cuff Wace when he dropped his pen.

It was almost as if he realized he hadn't much longer for this life.

Nigel Kilby was already awake when the school bell rang at half-past seven the next morning. He jumped out of bed, put on his spectacles and ran over to the radiator on top of which he had left his lethal mixture to mature. He noted with satisfaction that it had turned into a grayish paste. He held it to his nose and sniffed, and decided that it smelled of shoe polish, but not too strongly.

Twenty minutes later the first bell rang for breakfast. In the dining hall where they sat by forms, middle school was at one end of the room. This meant that the boys on one side had their backs against a wall and those sitting on the opposite side had theirs turned to the rest of the room, which provided Kilby with as much cover as he could hope to have when the crucial moment arrived.

Before leaving the dormitory, he had transferred the mixture to a paper bag which he put in his trouser pocket.

"How much are you going to give him?" Wace had asked.

"I reckon it's so deadly, it won't need much."

"How are you going go sprinkle it on?" Perry mi had inquired earnestly. "It looks all sticky."

"I'll just put in a few bits. If Cheesepot comes back too soon, you'll have to kick me under the table, Marsden."

"Aren't you frightened of getting some on your own plate, Kilby?" someone else had asked.

He shook his head. "I shall be extra careful and wash my hands as soon as breakfast is over."

The novelty of this struck silence into his audience and a couple of minutes later the second bell rang and they trooped downstairs to the dining hall.

Mr. Cheeseman came in late, just as the headmaster was starting to say grace. He gave the boys a curt nod and began ladling out the porridge. He was never very communicative at breakfast, but this morning there seemed something subtly different about him. Nothing which could be called an improvement, but nevertheless different. His eyes looked as they did when he had a hangover, but there wasn't the usual smell that went with that condition. He had a grimly brooding air.

Kilby wondered whether others had noticed the difference as he watched Mr. Cheeseman through his own quite different eyes. The eyes of an executioner.

When each boy had been served, Mr. Cheeseman filled his own bowl and then, as they had hoped, stalked away to the table presided over by Mr. Saunders.

Kilby had given the strictest instructions that, when this moment was reached, everyone must eat normally and not gaze up the table in his direction, as this could give the whole thing away. Despite the warning, he observed Wace leaning forward and staring at him as though about to witness a conjuring trick. He gave him a furious glare at the same time as Webster kicked him on the ankle. Wace blushed and quickly picked up his spoon.

Removing the crumpled paper bag from his pocket, Kilby slid to the very end of the bench so that his movements would be masked from everyone save those of his own form on the opposite side of the table. Quickly he shook out four pellets of the gray paste on to the waiting plate, where they promptly sank from sight beneath the surface of equally gray porridge.

He was halfway through his own porridge before Mr. Cheeseman returned to the table and sat down. With twelve pairs of eyes trying not to stare at him, be began to eat. At one moment, he made a face and appeared to remove something from the tip of his tongue, but otherwise he ate without comment. Porridge was followed by kippers and the meal ended with a slice of bread and margarine, covered by a film of marmalade.

There was a grating noise as the headmaster pushed back his chair and said, "I'll say grace for those who've finished."

This was followed by a noisy exodus, leaving only the dreamers and slow eaters to continue chewing their wholesome cud.

Mr. Cheeseman had left with the majority without having spoken a single word during the meal. Kilby was puzzled and Perry mi voiced the theory that their form master had already had a vision of the angel of death.

"How long will it take to work?" Webster asked as he and Kilby went out of the dining hall together.

Kilby shrugged noncommittally. "Difficult to say."

"I hope it means we miss French."

As events turned out, they missed History as well.

History should have been the first lesson of the day and at twenty to nine, five minutes before it was due to start, middle school were at their desks.

"I wonder if he'll come out in spots first," Wace whispered to Webster.

"I don't want to see him actually die in here," Webster said with a slight shiver.

Noise from other classrooms along the corridor began to die away, indicating the arrival of teachers for the start of the day's work. But there was no sign of Mr. Cheeseman. A quarter to nine came and went. Then ten to nine and five to nine. But still no Cheesepot.

"It must have worked already," Marsden said in a hoarse whisper, and Kilby swallowed nervously. "I mean, he's never been as late as this before. What are we going to do?"

"If he hasn't come by the time the school clock strikes nine, I'll go and have a look around," Kilby said.

It seemed no time at all before nine o'clock struck, hurling them into a state of high tension such as they had never experienced.

Kilby rose from his desk. "Everyone stay here. If anyone comes, say I've gone to look for Cheesepot."

He slipped out of the classroom, half-closing the door behind him. It was doubtful whether middle school had ever sat in silence for so long. Even Webster and Wace barely exchanged a whispered word.

It was a quarter of an hour before Kilby returned and they could see at once from his expression that something had happened. His face was white and he kept on blinking behind his spectacles. With great deliberation, he moistened his lips.

"He's dead all right," he announced in a quavering voice. "He's lying on the floor of the mower shed."

The news was greeted in stunned silence, apart from a few quick gasps. Deliverance had come, but their reaction was not as they had anticipated. There was no urge to cheer or bang their desk tops, just a feeling of fearful unease.

Perry mi was the first to break the silence.

"Did you feel his pulse?" he asked.

Kilby shook his head. "I didn't go into the shed. I looked

through the keyhole and could see him lying there in a sort of heap."

"How do you know it was Cheesepot?" Marsden asked.

"I could tell by his jacket. The black and white check one he was wearing at breakfast. He must have been bending over the mower when he collapsed."

"He might have still been breathing," Perry mi remarked in a worried tone.

"No, he was dead all right. I'd have noticed if he was breathing. His chest would have been going up and down."

"What are we going to do?" Wace asked, a note of panic in his voice.

The question was answered for them by the sudden appearance in the doorway of Mr. Repping, the headmaster.

"What are you all doing?" he asked sharply. "Where's Mr. Cheeseman?"

"We don't know, sir," Kilby replied. "He hasn't turned up."

"Hasn't turned up! But he was at breakfast."

"Yes, sir," agreed a chorus of voices.

"Well, get on with some work while I go and find out what's happened. Now, no talking, do you understand?"

"May I make a suggestion, sir?" Kilby said.

"Well, what is it, Kilby?"

"Mr. Cheeseman often goes to the mower shed between breakfast and first period, sir."

"I'm aware of that, Kilby."

"Sorry, sir, I just thought it might be a good idea to look there. He might have had an accident and be trapped."

Mr. Repping frowned. "That sounds most far-fetched. You're letting your imagination run away with you, Kilby. Now, get on with your work while I go and attend to the matter."

It was half an hour before the headmaster returned. Half an hour during which the minutes ticked away with agonizing slowness and very little work was done. When he did reappear in the classroom, they stared at him in fascinated horror while waiting to hear how he would break the news.

"Well, I'm afraid the mystery remains unsolved for the time being," he said briskly. "I've tried to phone Mr. Cheeseman's home, but can't get any answer, so both he and Mrs. Cheeseman must be out. I believe Mr. Price is free next period so I'll ask him to come and take you. What is your next period by the way?"

"French, sir," Marsden said when no one else spoke.

"Very well, stay in your classroom and I'll go and speak to Mr. Price."

"Excuse me, sir."

"Yes, what is it, Kilby?"

"Didn't you look in the mower shed, sir?"

"As a matter of fact, I did, Kilby. I told you that you were letting your imagination run away with you, lad. There wasn't a single sign of Mr. Cheeseman having been in there this morning."

Fifty minutes of French with the benign Mr. Price would normally have been something of a treat, but middle school agreed afterwards that they had never known the clock to move so slowly. It seemed as if the mid-morning break would never come. And when at last it did, Nigel Kilby found himself facing a barrage of questions which would have undermined the confidence of anyone less self-assured. As it was, however, he stuck to his story and remained outwardly unshaken. Cheesepot had definitely been lying on the floor beside the mower, his black and white check jacket being unmistakable. If he was no longer there when Mr. Repping inspected the shed, it meant only one thing. His body had been removed.

"But who'd have done it, Kilby?"

"And why, Kilby?"

To these and similar questions, Nigel Kilby did not pretend to have answers, but his trump card which he played over and over again was to remind his audience that Cheesepot had indisputably disappeared.

"Body-snatching is not unknown," he added in a tone

125

which hinted at personal experience of the practice.

And so the day dragged by with Mr. Cheeseman's twelve jurors fermenting in an agony of feverish speculation.

When bedtime came, still without any news of their form master, the prospect of sleep could not have seemed more distant.

It was Perry mi who suggested that, like a wild animal aware of its approaching end, Cheesepot had gone off to die in a cave. But Kilby crushed this theory by pointing out that it didn't begin to fit the facts.

"I wish now we'd never sentenced him to death," Wace whispered to Webster in the next bed.

"So do I," Webster said. "I'm scared."

At breakfast the next morning, the head boy was deputed to sit at the end of their table and serve the porridge. He and Marsden then spent the whole time discussing England's cricket prospects in the coming season.

When breakfast was over, various masters were to be observed exchanging conspiratorial whispers, but of Mr. Cheeseman there was neither sign nor mention.

By twenty minutes to nine, middle school were sitting at their desks wondering what to expect. Their first lesson was Latin and it seemed possible that the headmaster himself might take it.

Kilby had reminded them all of the need to stand firm and not break ranks because they had all been in it together. Anyone who sneaked could expect a fate little better than Cheesepot's.

"What have you done with the rest of the poison?" Perry mi asked.

"I flushed it down the lav last night," Kilby replied.

The sound of approaching footsteps in the corridor brought them to silence and a moment later the headmaster entered, followed by a stranger. He was dressed in a tweed suit and had an outdoor appearance. To Kilby, he looked much more like a farmer than a teacher. Though teacher he must presumably be.

126

Mr. Repping mounted the dais and clutched both sides of the high desk in front of him. The stranger stood at his side letting his gaze roam impassively over the two rows of faces. He had blue eyes which gave the impression of missing nothing. He certainly didn't look to be a tyrant in the same mold as Cheesepot; equally, he didn't give the appearance of being a soft touch.

This line of thought was passing through a number of heads as the boys sought to assess him. Thus the jolt they received when the headmaster spoke was like a severe electric shock.

"Boys, this is Detective Inspector Cartwright. He has some questions he wants to ask you about Mr. Cheeseman's disappearance and I expect you to be completely truthful in your answers." He turned to the officer. "I shall be in my study if you want me, Inspector." Glancing back at the two rows of anxious upturned faces, he added, "Inspector Cartwright has said that he would like to speak to you alone. That's why I'm leaving the classroom. But he'll certainly report to me if anyone misbehaves."

Inspector Cartwright watched Mr. Repping's departure and waited for the door to be closed. Then he looked at the boys and gave them a broad wink.

"You look just like a jury sitting there," he said in an amused tone. Kilby gulped and several other boys blushed, all of which he observed. "As the headmaster told you, I want to ask you some questions about Mr. Cheeseman. When did you last see him?"

"At breakfast yesterday, sir," Kilby said when no one else answered.

"That would have been at eight o'clock. Right? And he never turned up for your first lesson at eight forty-five, is that right?"

"Yes, sir," Kilby said, while others nodded.

"Did anyone go and look for him?" Inspector Cartwright became aware that no one was looking at him any longer, all eyes having become suddenly cast down. "Didn't anyone go looking for him? Surely it would have been quite a natural thing to do?"

"I did, sir," Kilby said at the end of an oppressive silence.

"What's your name?"

"Kilby, sir."

"Where did you go and look, Kilby?"

"The shed where the mower's kept, sir."

"Ah! That would explain why you urged Mr. Repping to look there, eh? And what did you discover?"

Kilby swallowed hard and then met Inspector Cartwright's gaze full on. "I saw his body, sir, when I looked through the keyhole. He was lying in a heap beside the mower. I knew it was him, sir, because I recognized his jacket."

"It must have given you quite a shock, eh?"

"Yes, sir."

"But it didn't come as a total surprise?"

"Sir?"

"Seeing him dead on the shed floor?"

Even Kilby felt defenceless in the face of this *deus ex machina*.

"No, sir," he said in a faint whisper.

"Not a very popular master, I gather?"

"No, sir."

"Did anyone like him?" He glanced from boy to boy as he spoke.

"He was the most unpopular master in the whole of England, sir," Perry mi broke in.

Inspector Cartwright received this news with pursed lips and a thoughtful nod.

"It must be a relief to you to know he won't be teaching you anymore." He paused. "Well, I think that's about all ... unless anyone has a question to ask me."

Everyone looked toward Kilby who appeared to be fighting some inner battle.

"Have you found the body yet, sir?" he blurted out at last.

Inspector Cartwright looked solemn. "Yes, it was down a crevice at the top of the cliffs. We'd never have discovered it if we hadn't been told."

"But who put it there, sir?"

"Whose body are we talking about?" Inspector Cartwright inquired in a tone of mock puzzlement.

"Mr. Cheeseman's, sir," half a dozen voices called out.

"Oh! Oh, his body's at the police station."

"Then whose body was it on the cliff, sir?" Kilby asked in a bewildered voice.

"Mrs. Cheeseman's."

"Is she dead, too?"

"Hers is the only body I know about."

"But I thought you said, sir, that Mr. Cheeseman . . ."

"Is at the police station, charged with the murder of his wife. We picked him up outside Dover last night. He and his lady friend were about to cross the Channel, but he was recognized when he went into a chemist's shop. It seems he'd had horrible griping pains in his stomach all day. But for that, he'd almost certainly have got away." Inspector Cartwright's eye had a strange glint as he went on: "As it is, he has told us everything, including how he placed an old bolster dressed in his jacket and trousers in the mower shed, which he removed as soon as he'd seen Kilby look through the keyhole. He reckoned that if he and his lady friend could disappear abroad and his wife's body was never found, the mystery would never be solved. The assumption would be that his wife had murdered him and then vanished. But those tummy pains were his undoing. And all because he underestimated your ability to make the porridge nastier than I'm sure it is." Inspector Cartwright stepped off the dais as if to go, then paused. "I'd like to offer you boys just two bits of advice. The first is not to take the law into your own hands and the second is, if you do, make sure your intended victim doesn't overhear your plans."

He reached the door and paused again. "But as things have turned out, you seem to have gained the best of both worlds. Got rid of a bully of a master and helped the police catch a murderer."

THE CROSS OF LORRAINE

ISAAC ASIMOV

Isaac Asimov is best known for his science fiction, but his great inventiveness led him to try other forms as well, including the detective story.

And the number of variations that can be played on the detective theme is infinite. Here, for example, Asimov's genial group of friends the Black Widowers confront a detective story without a crime: how can someone disappear without a trace? There is a clue, but the clue itself seems to have disappeared. Even a trained observer like a magician can't see it.

EMMANUEL RUBIN did not, as a general rule, ever permit a look of relief to cross his face. Had one done so, it would have argued a prior feeling of uncertainty or apprehension, sensations he might feel but would certainly never admit to.

This time, however, the relief was unmistakable. It was monthly banquet time for the Black Widowers. Rubin was the host and it was he who was supplying the guest. And here it was twenty minutes after seven and only now—with but ten minutes left before dinner was to start—only now did his guest arrive.

Rubin bounded toward him, careful, however, not to spill a drop of his second drink.

"Gentlemen," he said, clutching the arm of the newcomer, "my guest, The Amazing Larri—spelled L-A-R-R-I." And in a lowered voice, over the hum of pleased-to-meet-yous, "Where the hell were you?"

Larri muttered, "The subway train stalled." Then he returned smiles and greetings.

"Pardon me," said Henry, the perennial—and nonpareil—waiter at the Black Widower banquets, "but there is not much time for the guest to have his drink before dinner begins. Would you state your preference, sir?"

"A good notion, that," said Larri gratefully. "Thank you, waiter, and let me have a dry martini, but not too darned dry —a little damp, so to speak."

"Certainly, sir," said Henry.

Rubin said, "I've told you, Larri, that we members all have our *ex officio* doctorates, so now let me introduce them in nauseating detail. This tall gentleman with the neat mustache, black eyebrows, and straight back is Dr. Geoffrey Avalon. He's a lawyer and he never smiles. The last time he tried, he was fined for contempt of court."

Avalon smiled as broadly as he could and said, "You undoubtedly know Manny well enough, sir, not to take him seriously."

"Undoubtedly," said Larri. As he and Rubin stood together, they looked remarkably alike. Both were the same height— about five feet five—both had active, inquisitive faces, both had straggly beards, though Larri's was longer and was accompanied by a fringe of hair down both sides of his face as well.

Rubin said, "And here, dressed fit to kill anyone with a real taste for clothing, is our artist-expert, Dr. Mario Gonzalo, who will insist on producing a caricature of you in which he will claim to see a resemblance. —Dr. Roger Halsted inflicts pain on junior high-school students under the guise of teaching them what little he knows of mathematics. —Dr. James Drake

131

is a superannuated chemist who once conned someone into granting him a Ph.D. —And finally, Dr. Thomas Trumbull, who works for the government in an unnamed job as a code expert and who spends most of his time hoping Congress doesn't find out."

"Manny," said Trumbull wearily, "if it were possible to cast a retroactive blackball, I think you could count on five."

And Henry said, "Gentlemen, dinner is served."

It was one of those rare Black Widower occasions when lobster was served, rarer now than ever because of the increase in price.

Rubin, who as host bore the cost, shrugged it off. "I made a good paperback sale last month and we can call this a celebration."

"We can celebrate," said Avalon, "but lobster tends to kill conversation. The cracking of claws and shells, the extraction of meat, the dipping in melted butter—all that takes one's full concentration." And he grimaced with the effort he was putting into the compression of a nutcracker.

"In that case," said the Amazing Larri, "I shall have a monopoly of the conversation," and he grinned with satisfaction as a large platter of prime rib-roast was dexterously placed before him by Henry.

"Larri is allergic to seafood," said Rubin.

Conversation was indeed subdued, as Avalon had predicted, until the various lobsters had been clearly worsted in culinary battle, and then, finally, Halsted asked, "What makes you Amazing, Larri?"

"Stage name," said Larri. "I am a prestidigitator, an escapist extraordinary, and the greatest living exposer."

Trumbull, who was sitting to Larri's right, formed ridges on his bronzed forehead. "What the devil do you mean by 'exposer'?"

Rubin beat a tattoo on his water glass at this point and said, "No grilling till we've had our coffee."

"For God's sake," said Trumbull, "I'm just asking for the

definition of a word."

"Host's decision is final," said Rubin.

Trumbull scowled in Rubin's direction. "Then I'll guess the answer. An exposer is one who exposes fakes—people who, using trickery of one sort or another, pretend to produce effects they attribute to supernatural or paranatural forces."

Larri thrust out his lower lip, raised his eyebrows, and nodded. "Very good for a guess. I couldn't have put it better."

Gonzalo said, "You mean that whatever someone did by what he claimed was real magic, you could do by stage magic?"

"Exactly," said Larri. "For instance, suppose that some mystic claimed he had the capacity to bend spoons by means of unknown forces. I can do the same by using natural force, this way." He lifted his spoon and, holding it by its two ends, he bent it half an inch out of shape.

Trumbull said, "That scarcely counts. Anyone can do it that way."

"Ah," said Larri, "but this spoon you saw me bend is not the amazing effect at all. That spoon you were watching merely served to trap and focus the ethereal rays that did the real work. Those rays acted to bend *your* spoon, Dr. Trumbull."

Trumbull looked down and picked up his spoon, which was bent nearly at right angles. "How did you do this?"

Larri shrugged. "Would you believe ethereal forces?"

Drake laughed, and pushing his dismantled lobster toward the center of the table, lit a cigarette. He said, "Larri did it a few minutes ago, with his hands, when you weren't looking."

Larri seemed unperturbed by exposure. "When Manny banged his glass, Dr. Trumbull, you looked away. I had rather hoped you all would."

Drake said, "I know better than to pay attention to Manny."

"But," said Larri, "if no one had seen me do it, would you have accepted the ethereal forces?"

"Not a chance," said Trumbull.

"Even if there had been no other way in which you could

explain the effect?—Here, let me show you something. Suppose you wanted to flip a coin—"

He fell silent for a moment while Henry passed out the strawberry shortcake, pushed his own serving out of the way, and said, "Suppose you wanted to flip a coin without actually lifting it and turning it—this penny, for instance. There are a number of ways it could be done. The simplest would be merely to touch it quickly, because, as you all know, a finger is always slightly sticky, especially at meal time, so that the coin lifts up slightly as the finger is removed and can easily be made to flip over. It is tails now, you see. Touch it again and it is heads."

Gonzalo said, "No prestidigitation there, though. We see it flip."

"Exactly," said Larri, "and that's why I won't do it that way. Let's put something over it so that it can't be touched. Suppose we use a—" He looked around the table for a moment and seized a salt shaker. "Suppose we use this."

He placed the salt shaker over the coin and said, "Now it's showing heads—"

"Hold on," said Gonzalo. "How do we know it's showing heads? It could be tails and then, when you reveal it later, you'll say it flipped, when it was tails all along."

"You're perfectly right," said Larri, "and I'm glad you raised the point. —Dr. Drake, you have eyes that caught me before. Would you check this on behalf of the assembled company? I'll lift the salt shaker and you tell me what the coin shows."

Drake looked and said, "Heads," in his softly hoarse voice.

"You'll all take Dr. Drake's word, I hope, gentlemen?— Please, watch me place the salt shaker back on the coin and make sure it doesn't flip in the process—"

"It didn't," said Drake.

"Now to keep my fingers from slipping while performing this trick, I will put this paper napkin over the salt shaker."

Larri folded the paper napkin neatly and carefully around the salt shaker, then said, "But, in manipulating this napkin, I

caused you all to divert your attention from the penny and you may think I have flipped it in the process." He lifted the salt shaker with the napkin around it, and said, "Dr. Drake, will you check the coin again?"

Drake leaned toward it. "Still heads," he said.

Very carefully and gently Larri put back the salt shaker, the paper napkin still folded around it, and said, "The coin remained as is?"

"Still heads," said Drake.

"In that case, I now perform the magic." Larri pushed down on the salt shaker and the paper napkin collapsed. There was nothing inside.

There was a moment of shock, and then Gonzalo said, "Where's the salt shaker?"

"In another plane of existence," said Larri airily.

"But you said you were going to flip the coin."

"I lied."

Avalon said, "There's no mystery. He had us all concentrating on the coin as a diversion tactic. When he picked up the salt shaker with the napkin around it to let Jim look at the coin, he just dropped the salt shaker into his hand and placed the empty, folded napkin over the coin."

"Did you see me do that, Dr. Avalon?" asked Larri.

"No. I was looking at the coin, too."

"Then you're just guessing," said Larri.

Rubin, who had not participated in the demonstration at all, but who had eaten his strawberry shortcake instead, said, "The tendency is to argue these things out logically and that's impossible. Scientists and other rationalists are used to dealing with the universe, which fights fair. Faced with a mystic who does not, they find themselves maneuvered into believing nonsense and, in the end, making fools of themselves.

"Magicians, on the other hand," Rubin went on, "know what to watch for, are experienced enough not to be misdirected, and are not impressed by the apparently supernatural. That's why mystics generally won't perform if they know magicians are in the audience."

Coffee had been served and was being sipped, and Henry was quietly preparing the brandy, when Rubin sounded the water glass and said, "Gentlemen, it is time for the official grilling, assuming you idiots have left anything to grill. Jeff, will you do the honors tonight?"

Avalon cleared his throat portentously and frowned down on The Amazing Larri from under his dark and luxuriant eyebrows. Using his voice in the deepest of its naturally deep register, he said, "It is customary to ask our guests to justify their existences, but if today's guest exposes phony mystics even occasionally, I, for one, consider his existence justified and will pass on to another question.

"The temptation is to ask you how you performed your little disappearing trick of a few moments ago, but I quite understand that the ethics of your profession preclude your telling us—even though everything said here is considered under the rose, and though nothing has ever leaked, I will refrain from that question.

"Let me instead ask about your failures. —Sir, you describe yourself as an exposer. Have there been any supposedly mystical demonstrations you have not been able to account for by natural means?"

Larri said, "I have not attempted to explain all the effects I have ever encountered or heard of, but where I have studied an effect and made an attempt to duplicate it, I have succeeded in every case."

"No failures?"

"None."

Avalon considered that, but as he prepared for the next question, Gonzalo broke in. His head was leaning on one palm, but the fingers of that hand were carefully disposed in such a way as not to disarray his hair. He said, "Now, wait, Larri, would it be right to suggest that you tackled only easy cases? The really puzzling cases you might have made no attempts to explain?"

"You mean," said Larri, "that I shied away from anything

that might spoil my perfect record or that might upset my belief in the rational order of the universe?—If so, you're quite wrong, Dr. Gonzalo. Most reports of apparent mystical powers are dull and unimportant, crude and patently false. I ignore those. The cases I do take on are precisely the puzzling ones that have attracted attention because of their unusual nature and their apparent divorce from the rational. So, you see, the ones I take on are precisely those you suspect I avoid."

Gonzalo subsided and Avalon said, "Larri, the mere fact that you can duplicate a trick by prestidigitation doesn't mean that it couldn't also have been performed by a mystic through supernatural means. The fact that human beings can build machines that fly doesn't mean that birds are man-made machines."

"Quite right," said Larri, "but mystics lay their claims to supernatural powers on the notion, either expressed or implicit, that there is no other way of producing the effect. If I show that the same effect *can* be produced by natural means, the burden of proof then shifts to them to show that the effect can be produced after the natural means are made impossible. I don't know of any mystic who has accepted the conditions set by professional magicians to guard against trickery and who then succeeded."

"And nothing has ever baffled you? Not even the tricks other magicians have developed?"

"Oh, yes, there are effects produced by some magicians that baffle me in the sense that I don't know quite how they do it. I might duplicate the effect by perhaps using a different method. In any case, that's not the point. As long as an effect is produced by natural means, it doesn't matter whether I can reproduce it or not. I am not the best magician in the world. I am just a better magician than any mystic is."

Halsted, his high forehead flushed, and stuttering slightly in his eagerness to speak, said, "But then nothing would startle you? No disappearance like the one involving the salt shaker?"

"You mean that one?" asked Larri, pointing. There was a

salt shaker in the middle of the table, but no one had seen it placed there.

Halsted, thrown off a moment, recovered and said, "Have you ever been *startled* by any disappearance? I heard once that magicians have made elephants disappear."

"Actually, making an elephant disappear is childishly simple. I assure you there's nothing puzzling about disappearances performed in a magic act." And then a peculiar look crossed Larri's face, a flash of sadness and frustration. "Not in a magic act. Just—"

"Yes?" said Halsted. "Just what?"

"Just in real life," said Larri, smiling and attempting to toss off the remark lightheartedly.

"Just a minute," said Trumbull, "we can't let that pass. If there has been a disappearance in real life you can't explain, we want to hear about it."

Larri shook his head. "No, no, Dr. Trumbull. It is not a mysterious disappearance or an inexplicable one. Nothing like that at all. I just—well, I lost something and can't find it and it—saddens me."

"The details," said Trumbull.

"It wouldn't be worth your attention," said Larri, embarrassed. "It's a—silly story and somewhat—" He fell into silence.

"Damn it," thundered Trumbull, "we all sit here and voluntarily refrain from asking anything that might result in your being tempted to violate your ethics. Would it violate the ethics of the magician's art for you to tell this story?"

"It's not that at all—"

"Well, then, sir, I repeat what Jeff has told you. Everything said here is in absolute confidence, and the agreement surrounding these monthly dinners is that all questions must be answered. —Manny?"

Rubin shrugged. "That's the way it is, Larri. If you don't want to answer the question we'll have to declare the meeting at an end."

Larri sat back in his chair and looked depressed. "I can't

very well allow that to happen, considering the fine hospitality I've been shown. I will tell you the story, but you'll find there's not much to it. I met a woman quite accidentally; I lost touch with her; I can't locate her. That's all there is."

"No," said Trumbull, "that's not all there is. Where and how did you meet her? Where and how did you lose touch with her? Why can't you find her again? We want to know the details."

Gonzalo said, "In fact, if you tell us the details, we may be able to help you."

Larri laughed sardonically. "I think not."

"You'd be surprised," said Gonzalo. "In the past—"

Avalon said, "Quiet, Mario. Don't make promises we might not be able to keep. —Would you give us the details, sir? I assure you we'll do our best to help."

Larri smiled wearily. "I appreciate your offer, but you will see that there is nothing you can do merely by sitting here."

He adjusted himself in his seat and said, "I was done with my performance in an upstate town—I'll give you the details when and if you insist, but for the moment they don't matter, except that this happened about a month ago. I had to get to another small town some hundred and fifty miles away for a morning show and that presented a little transportation problem.

"My magic, unfortunately, is not the kind that can transport me a hundred and fifty miles in a twinkling, or even conjure up a pair of seven-league boots. I did not have my car with me —just as well, for I don't like to travel strange roads at night when I am sleepy—and the net result was that I would have to take a bus that would take nearly four hours. I planned to catch some sleep while on wheels and thus make the trip serve a double purpose.

"But when things go wrong, they go wrong in battalions, so you can guess that I missed my bus and that the next one would not come along for two more hours. There was an enclosed station in which I could wait, one that was as dreary as you could imagine—with no reading matter except some fly-blown posters on the wall—no place to buy a paper or a cup of coffee. I thought grimly that it was fortunate it wasn't raining, and settled down to drowse, when my luck changed.

"A woman walked in. I've never been married, gentlemen, and I've never even had what young people today call a 'meaningful relationship'. Some casual attachments, perhaps, but on the whole, though it seems trite to say so, I am married to my art and find it much more satisfying than women, generally.

"I had no reason to think that this woman was an improvement on the generality, but she had a pleasant appearance. She was something over thirty, and was just plump enough to have a warm, comfortable look about her, and she wasn't too tall.

"She looked about and said, smiling, 'Well, I've missed my bus, I see.'

"I smiled with her. I liked the way she said it. She didn't fret or whine or act annoyed at the universe. It was a good-humored statement of fact, and just hearing it cheered me up tremendously because actually I myself was in the mood to fret and whine and act annoyed. Now I could be as good-natured as she and say, 'Two of us, madam, so you don't even have the satisfaction of being unique.'

" 'So much the better,' she said. 'We can talk and pass the time that much faster.'

"I was astonished. She did not treat me as a potential attacker or as a possible thief. God knows I am not handsome or even particularly respectable in appearance, but it was as though she had casually penetrated to my inmost character and found it satisfactory. You have no idea how flattered I was. If I were ten times as sleepy, I would have stayed up to talk to her.

"And we did talk. Inside of fifteen minutes I knew I was having the pleasantest conversation in my life—in a crummy bus station at midnight. I can't tell you all we talked about, but I can tell you what we *didn't* talk about. We didn't talk about magic.

"I can interest anyone by doing tricks, but then it isn't me they're interested in; it's the flying fingers and the patter they like. And while I'm willing to buy attention that way, you don't know how pleasant it is to get the attention without purchasing it. She apparently just liked to listen to me, and I know I liked to listen to her.

"Fortunately, my trip was not an all-out effort, so I didn't have my large trunk with the show-business advertising all over it, just two rather large valises. I told her nothing personal about myself, and asked nothing about her. I gathered briefly that she was heading for her brother's place, that it was right on the road, that she would have to wake him up because she had carelessly let herself be late—but she only told me that in order to say that she was glad it had happened. She would buy my company at the price of inconveniencing her brother. I liked that.

"We didn't talk politics or world affairs or religion or the theater. We talked people—all the funny and odd and peculiar things we had observed about people. We laughed for two hours, during which not one other person came to join us. I had never had anything like that happen to me, had never felt so alive and happy, and when the bus finally came at 1:50 A.M., it was amazing how sorry I was. I didn't want the night to end.

"When we got onto the bus, of course, it was no longer quite the same thing, even though we found a double seat we could share. After all, we had been alone in the station and there we could talk loudly and laugh. On the bus people were sleeping.

"Of course it wasn't all bad. It was a nice feeling to have her so close to me. Despite the fact that I'm rather an old horse, I felt like a teenager—enough like a teenager, in fact, to be embarrassed at being watched.

"Immediately across the way was a woman and her young son. He was about eight years old, I should judge, and *he* was awake. He kept watching me with his sharp little eyes. I could see those eyes fixed on us every time a streetlight shone into

142

the bus and it was very inhibiting. I wished he were asleep but, of course, the excitement of being on a bus, perhaps, was keeping him awake.

"The motion of the bus, the occasional whisper, the feeling of being quite out of reality, the pressure of her body against mine—it was like confusing dream and fact, and the boundary between sleep and wakefulness just vanished. I didn't intend to sleep, and I started awake once or twice, but then finally, when I started awake one more time, it was clear there had been a considerable period of sleep, and the seat next to me was empty."

Halsted said, "I take it she had gotten off."

"I didn't think she had disappeared into thin air," said Larri. "Naturally, I looked about. I couldn't call her name, because I didn't know her name. She wasn't in the rest room, because its door was swinging open.

"The little boy across the aisle spoke in a rapid high treble— in French. I can understand French reasonably well, but I didn't have to make any effort, because his mother was now awakened and she translated. She spoke English quite well. She said, 'Pardon me, sir, but is it that you are looking for the woman that was with you?'

" 'Yes,' I said. 'Did you see where she got off?'

" 'Not I, sir. I was sleeping. But my son says that she descended at the place of the Cross of Lorraine.'

" 'At the what?'

"She repeated it, and so did the child, in French.

"She said, 'You must excuse my son, sir. He is a great hero worshipper of President Charles de Gaulle and though he is young he knows the tale of the Free French forces in the war very well. He would not miss a sight like a Cross of Lorraine. If he said he saw it, he did.'

"I thanked them and then went forward to the bus driver and asked him, but at that time of night the bus stops wherever a passenger would like to get off, or get on. He had made numerous stops and let numerous people on and off, and he didn't know for sure where he had stopped and whom he had let off. He was rather churlish, in fact."

Avalon cleared his throat. "He may have thought you were up to no good and was deliberately withholding information to protect the passenger."

"Maybe," said Larri despondently, "but what it amounted to was that I had lost her. When I came back to my seat, I found a little note tucked into the pocket of the jacket I had placed in the rack above. I managed to read it by a streetlight at the next stop, where the French mother and son got off. It said, 'Thank you so much for a delightful time. Gwendolyn.' "

Gonzalo said, "You have her first name anyway."

Larri said, "I would appreciate having had her last name, her address, her telephone number. A first name is useless."

"You know," said Rubin, "she may deliberately have withheld information because she wasn't interested in continuing the acquaintanceship. A romantic little interlude is one thing; a continuing danger is another. She may be a married woman."

"Have you done anything about trying to find her?" asked Gonzalo.

"Certainly," said Larri sardonically. "If a magician is faced with a disappearing woman he must understand what has happened. I have gone over the bus route twice by car, looking for a Cross of Lorraine. If I had found it, I would have gone in and asked if anyone there knew a woman by the name of Gwendolyn. I'd have described her. I'd have gone to the local post office or the local police station."

"But you haven't found a Cross of Lorraine, I take it," said Trumbull.

"I have not."

Halsted said, "Mathematically speaking, it's a finite problem. You could try every post office along the whole route."

Larri sighed. "If I get desperate enough, I'll try. But, mathematically speaking, that would be so inelegant. Why can't I find the Cross of Lorraine?"

"The youngster might have made a mistake," said Trumbull.

"Not a chance," said Larri. "An adult, yes, but a child, never. Adults have accumulated enough irrationality to be very unreliable eyewitnesses. A bright eight-year-old is different. Don't try to pull any trick on a bright kid; he'll see through it.

"Just the same," he went on, "nowhere on the route is there a restaurant, a department store, or anything else with the name Cross of Lorraine. I've checked every set of yellow pages along the entire route."

"Now wait awhile," said Avalon, "that's wrong. The child wouldn't have seen the words because they would have meant nothing to him. If he spoke and read only French, as I suppose he did, he would know the phrase as 'Croix de Lorraine.' The English would have never caught his eyes. He must have seen the symbol, the cross with the two horizontal bars, like this." He reached out and Henry obligingly handed him a menu.

Avalon turned it over and on the blank back drew the following:

"Actually," he said, "it's more properly called the Patriarchal Cross or the Archiepiscopal Cross since it symbolized the high office of patriarchs and archbishops by doubling the bars. You will not be surprised to hear that the Papal Cross has three bars. The Patriarchal Cross was used as a symbol of Godfrey of Bouillon, who was one of the leaders of the First Crusade, and since he was Duke of Lorraine, it came to be called the Cross of Lorraine. As we all know, it was adopted as the emblem of the Free French during the Hitlerian War." He coughed slightly and tried to look modest.

Larri said, a little impatiently, "I understand about the symbol, Dr. Avalon, and I didn't expect the youngster to note words. I think you'll agree, though, that any establishment calling itself the Cross of Lorraine would surely display the symbol along with the name. I looked for the name in the yellow pages and for the symbol on the road."

"And you didn't find it?" said Gonzalo.

"As I've already said, I didn't. I was desperate enough to consider things I didn't think the kid could possibly have seen at night. I thought, who knows how sharp young eyes are and how readily they may see something that represents an overriding interest? So I looked at signs in windows, at street signs—even at graffiti."

"If it were a graffito," said Trumbull, "which happens to be the singular form of graffiti, by the way, then, of course, it could have been erased between the time the child saw it and the time you came to look for it."

"I'm not sure of that," said Rubin. "It's my experience that graffiti are never erased. We've got some on the outside of our apartment house—"

"That's New York," said Trumbull. "In smaller towns there's less tolerance for these evidences of anarchy."

"Hold on," said Gonzalo, "what make you think graffiti are necessarily signs of anarchy? As a matter of fact—"

"Gentlemen! Gentlemen!" And as always, when Avalon's voice was raised to its full baritone, a silence fell. "We are not here to argue the merits and demerits of graffiti. The question is: how can we find this woman who disappeared? Larri has found no restaurant or other establishment with the name of Cross of Lorraine; he has found no evidence of the symbol along the route taken. Can we help him?"

Drake held up his hand and squinted through the curling smoke of his cigarette. "Hold on, there's no problem. Have you ever seen a Russian Orthodox Church? Do you know what its cross is like?" He made quick marks on the back of the menu and shoved it toward the center of the table. "Here —"

He said, "The kid, being hipped on the Free French, would take a quick look at that and see it as the Cross of Lorraine. So what you have to do, Larri, is look for a Russian Orthodox Church en route. I doubt there would be more than one."

Larri thought about it, but did not seem overjoyed. "The cross with that second bar set at an angle would be on the top of the spire, wouldn't it?"

"I imagine so."

"And it wouldn't be floodlit, would it? How would the child be able to see it at three or four o'clock in the morning?"

Drake stubbed out his cigarette. "Well, now, churches usually have a bulletin board near the entrance. There could have been a Russian Orthodox cross on the—"

"I would have seen it," said Larri firmly.

"Could it have been a Red Cross?" asked Gonzalo feebly. "You know, there might be a Red Cross headquarters along the route."

"The Red Cross," said Rubin, "is a Greek Cross with all four arms equal. I don't see how that could possibly be mistaken for a Cross of Lorraine by a Free French enthusiast. Look at it—"

Halsted said, "The logical thing, I suppose, is that you simply missed it, Larri. If you insist that, as a magician, you're such a trained observer that you *couldn't* have missed it, then maybe it was a symbol on something movable—on a truck in a driveway, for instance—and it moved on after sunrise."

"The boy made it quite clear that it was at the *place* of the Cross of Lorraine," said Larri. "I suppose even an eight-year-old can tell the difference between a place and a movable object."

"He spoke French. Maybe you mistranslated."

"I'm not that bad at the language," said Larri, "and besides, his mother translated and French is her native tongue."

"But English isn't. She might have gotten it wrong. The kid might have said something else. He might not even have said the Cross of Lorraine at all."

Avalon raised his hand for silence and said, "One moment, gentlemen, I see Henry, our esteemed waiter, smiling. What is it, Henry?"

Henry, from his place at the sideboard, said, "I'm afraid that I am amused at your doubting the child's evidence. It is quite certain, in my opinion, that he did see the Cross of Lorraine."

There was a moment's silence and Larri said, "How can you tell that, Henry?"

"By not being too subtle, sir."

Avalon's voice boomed out. "I knew it! We're being too complicated. Henry, how is it possible for us to achieve greater simplicity?"

"Why, Mr. Avalon, the incident took place at night. Instead of looking at all signs, all places, all varieties of cross, why not begin by asking ourselves what very few things *can* be easily seen on a highway at night?"

"A Cross of Lorraine?" asked Gonzalo incredulously.

"Certainly," said Henry, "among other things. Especially if we don't call it a Cross of Lorraine. What the youngster saw as a Cross of Lorraine, out of his special interest, we would see as something else so clearly that its relationship to the Cross of Lorraine would be invisible. What has been happening just now has been precisely what happened earlier with Mr. Larri's trick with the coin and the salt shaker. We concentrated on the coin and didn't watch the salt shaker, and now we concentrate on the Cross of Lorraine and don't look for the alternative."

Trumbull said, "Henry, if you don't stop talking in riddles, you're fired. What the hell is the Cross of Lorraine, if it isn't the Cross of Lorraine?"

Henry said gravely, "What is this?" and carefully he drew on the back of the menu—

Trumbull said, "A Cross of Lorraine—tilted."

"No, sir, you would never have thought so, if we hadn't been talking about the Cross of Lorraine. Those are English letters and a very common symbol on highways if you add something to it—" He wrote quickly and the tilted Cross became:

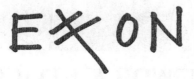

"The one thing," said Henry, "that is designed to be seen without trouble, day or night, on any highway, is a gas-station sign. The child saw the Cross of Lorraine in this one, but Mr. Larri, retracing the route, sees only a double X, since he reads the entire sign as Exxon. All signs showing this name, whether on the highway, in advertisements, or on credit cards, show the name in this fashion."

Now Larri caught fire. "You mean, Henry, that if I go into the Exxon stations en route and ask for Gwendolyn—"

"The proprietor of one of them is likely to be her brother, and there would not be more than a half dozen or so at most to inquire at."

"Good God, Henry," said Larri, "you're a magician."

"Merely simple-minded," said Henry, "though not, I hope, in the pejorative sense."

THE NEWDICK HELICOPTER

LESLIE CHARTERIS

Simon Templar, the Saint, is one of those characters everyone knows. He has featured in novels, short stories, comics, radio serials, television and movies; he is dashing, daring, handsome, sexy, rich, and never at a loss for a right uppercut or a witty remark.

He certainly solved crimes, but he was never a simple detective. He wasn't always on the side of the law—he was sometimes known as "The Robin Hood of Modern Crime"—but he was certainly on the side of the angels.

It's easy to forget how long he's been around. The first Saint stories were published in 1928, and he hasn't aged a day. This is one of the early Saint stories, from a time when helicopters—autogiros, as they were called then—were not as versatile as they are now. That didn't stop the Saint.

"I'M AFRAID," said Patricia Holm soberly, "you'll be getting into trouble again soon."

Simon Templar grinned, and opened another bottle of beer. He poured it out with a steady hand, unshaken by the future predicted for him.

"You may be right, darling," he admitted. "Trouble is one of the things that sort of happen to me, like other people have colds."

"I've often heard you complaining about it," said the

150

girl skeptically.

The Saint shook his head.

"You wrong me," he said. "Posterity will know me as a maligned, misunderstood, ill-used victim of a cruel fate. I have tried to be good. Instinctive righteousness glows from me like a inward light. But nobody gives it a chance. What do you suggest?"

"You might go into business."

"I know. Something safe and respectable, like manufacturing woollen combinations for elderly ladies with lorgnettes. We might throw in a pair of lorgnettes with every suit. You could knit them, and I'd do the fitting—the fitting of the lorgnettes, of course." Simon raised his glass and drank deeply. "It's an attractive idea, old darling, but all these schemes involve laying out a lot of capital on which you have to wait such a hell of a long time for a return. Besides, there can't be much of a profit in it. On a rough estimate, the amount of wool required to circumnavigate a fifty-four-inch bust—"

Monty Hayward, who was also present, took out a tobacco pouch and began to fill his pipe.

"I had some capital once," he said reminiscently, "but it didn't do me much good."

"How much can you lend me?" asked the Saint hopefully.

Monty brushed stray ends of tobacco from his lap and tested the draft through his handiwork cautiously.

"I haven't got it anymore, but I don't think I'd lend it to you if I had," he said kindly. "Anyway, the point doesn't arise because a fellow called Oscar Newdick has got it. Didn't I ever tell you about that?"

The Saint moved his head negatively, and settled deeper into his chair.

"It doesn't sound like you, Monty. D'you mean to say you were hornswoggled?"

Monty nodded.

"I suppose you might call it that. It happened about six years ago, when I was a bit younger and not quite so wise. It wasn't a bad swindle on the whole, though." He struck a match and puffed meditatively. "This fellow Newdick was a bloke I met on the train coming down from the office. He used to get into the same compartment with me three or four times a week, and naturally we took to passing the time of day— you know the way one does. He was an aeronautical engineer and a bit of an inventor, apparently. He was experimenting with autogiros, and he had a little one-horse factory near Walton where he was building them. He used to talk a lot of technical stuff about them to me, and I talked technical stuff about make-up and dummies to him—I don't suppose either of us understood half of what the other was talking about, so we got on famously."

With his pipe drawing satisfactorily, Monty possessed himself of the beer opener and executed a neat flanking movement toward the source of supply.

"Well, one day this fellow Newdick asked me if I'd like to drop over and have a look at his autogiros, so the following Saturday afternoon I hadn't anything particular to do and I took a run out to his aerodrome to see how he was getting along. All he had there was a couple of corrugated-iron sheds and a small field which he used to take off from and land at, but he really had got a helicopter effect which he said he'd made himself. He told me all about it and how it worked, which was all double-Dutch to me; and then he asked me if I'd like to go up in it. So I said 'Thank you very much, I should simply hate to go up in it.' You know what these things look like—an ordinary airplane with the wings taken off and just a sort of large fan business to hold you up in the air—I never have thought they looked particularly safe even when they're properly made, and I certainly didn't feel like risking my neck in this homemade version that he'd rigged up out of odd bits of wood and angle iron. However, he was so insistent about it and seemed so upset when I refused that eventually I thought I'd better gratify the old boy and just keep on praying that the damn thing wouldn't fall to pieces before we got down again."

The Saint sighed.

"So that's what happened to your face," he remarked, in a tone of profound relief. "If you only knew how that had been bothering me—"

"My mother did that," said Monty proudly. "No—we didn't crash. In fact, I had a really interesting flight. Either it must have been a very good machine, or he was a very good flier, because he made it do almost everything except answer questions. I don't know if you've ever been up in one of these autogiros—I've never been up in any other make, but this one was certainly everything that he claimed for it. It went up exactly like going up in a lift, and came down the same way. I never have known anything about the mechanics of these things, but after having had a ride in this bus of his I couldn't help feeling that the Air Age had arrived—I mean, anyone with a reasonable-sized lawn could have kept one of 'em and gone tootling off for weekends in it."

"And therefore," said the Saint reproachfully, "when he asked you if you'd like to invest some money in a company he was forming to turn out these machines and sell them at about twenty pounds a time, you hauled out your checkbook and asked him how much he wanted."

Monty chuckled good-humoredly.

"That's about it. The details don't really matter, but the fact is that about three weeks later I'd bought about five thousand quids' worth of shares."

"What was the catch?" Simon asked; and Monty shrugged.

"Well, the catch was simply that this heliocopter wasn't his invention at all. He had really built it himself, apparently, but it was copied line for line from one of the existing makes. There wasn't a thing in it that he'd invented. Therefore the design wasn't his, and he hadn't any right at all to manufacture it. So the company couldn't function. Of course, he didn't put it exactly like that. He told me that he'd 'discovered' that his designs 'overlapped' the existing patents —he swore that it was absolutely a coincidence, and nearly wept all over my office because his heart was broken because he'd found out that all his research work had already been done before. I told him I didn't believe a word of it, but that wasn't any help toward getting my money back. I hadn't any evidence against him that I could have brought into a court of law. Of course he'd told me that his design was patented and protected in every way, but he hadn't put any of that in writing, and when he came and told me the whole thing was smashed he denied it. He said he'd told me he was getting the design patented. I did see a solicitor about it afterwards, but he told me I hadn't a chance of proving a deliberate fraud. Newdick would probably have been ticked off in court for taking my money without reasonable precautions, but that wouldn't have brought any of it back."

"It was a private company, I suppose," said the Saint.

Monty nodded.

"If it had been a public one, with shares on the open market, it would have been a different matter," he said.

"What happened to the money?"

"Newdick had spent it—or he said he had. He told me he'd paid off all the old debts that had run up while he was experimenting, and spent the rest on some manufacturing plant and machinery for the company. He did give me about six or seven hundred back, and told me he'd work like hell to produce another invention that would really be original so he could pay me back the rest, but that was the last I heard of him. He's probably caught several other mugs with the same game since then." Monty grinned philosophically, looked at the clock, and got up. "Well, I must be getting along. I'll look in and see you on Saturday—if you haven't been arrested and shoved in clink before then."

He departed after another bottle of beer had been lowered; and when he had gone Patricia Holm viewed the Saint doubtfully. She had not missed the quiet attention with which he had followed Monty Hayward's narrative; and she had known Simon Templar a long time. The Saint had a fresh cigarette slanting from the corner of his mouth, his hands were in his pockets, and he was smiling at her with a seraphic innocence which was belied by every facet of the twinkling tang of mockery in his blue eyes.

"You know what I told you," she said.

He laughed.

"About getting into trouble? My darling, when will you stop thinking these wicked thoughts? I'm taking your advice to heart. Maybe there is something to be said for going into business. I think I should look rather fetching in a silk hat and a pair of white spats with pearl buttons; and you've no idea how I could liven up a directors' meeting if I set my mind to it."

Patricia was not convinced.

She was even less convinced when the Saint went out the next morning. From his extensive wardrobe he had selected one of his most elegant suits, a creation in light-hued saxony of the softest and most expensive weave—a garment which could by no possible chance have been worn by a man who had to devote his day to honest toil. His tie was dashing, his silk socks would have made a Communist's righteous indignation swell to bursting point, and over his right eye he had tilted a brand new Panama which would have made one wonder whether the strange shapeless headgear of the same breed worn by old gents while pottering around their gardens could conceivably be any relation whatsoever of such a superbly stylish lid. Moreover he had taken out the car which was the pride of his stable—the new cream and red Hirondel which was in itself the hallmark of a man who could afford to pay five thousand pounds for a car and thereafter watch a gallon of petrol blown into smoke every three or four miles.

"Where's the funeral?" she asked; and the Saint smiled blandly.

"I'm a young sportsman with far more money than sense, and I'm sure Comrade Newdick will be pleased to see me," he said; and he kissed her.

Mr. Oscar Newdick was pleased to see him—Simon Templar would have been vastly surprised if he hadn't been. That aura of idle affluence which the Saint could put on as easily as he put on a coat was one of his most priceless accessories, and it was never worn for any honest purpose.

But this Mr. Oscar Newdick did not know. To him, the arrival of such a person was like an answer to prayer. Monty Hayward's guess at Mr. Newdick's activities since collecting five thousand pounds from him was fairly accurate, but only fairly. Mr. Newdick had not caught several other mugs, but only three; and one of them had only been induced to invest a paltry three hundred pounds. The helicopter racket had been failing in its dividends, and the past year had not shown a single pennyworth of profit. Mr. Newdick did not believe in accumulating pennies: when he made a touch, it had to be a big one, and he was prepared to wait for it—the paltry three-hundred-pound investor had been an error of judgment, a young man who had grossly misled him with fabulous accounts of wealthy uncles, which when the time came to make the touch had been discovered to be the purest fiction— but recently the periods of waiting had exceeded all reasonable limits. Mr. Newdick had traveled literally thousands of miles on the more prosperous suburban lines in search of victims—the fellow-passenger technique really was his own invention, and he practiced it to perfection—but many moons had passed since he brought a prospective investor home from his many voyages.

When Simon Templar arrived, in fact, Mr. Newdick was gazing mournfully over the litter of spars and fabric and machinery in one of his corrugated-iron sheds, endeavoring to estimate its value in the junk market. The time had come, he was beginning to feel, when that particular stock-in-trade had paid the last percentage that could be squeezed out of it; it had rewarded him handsomely for his initial investment, but now it was obsolete. The best solution appeared to be to turn it in and concentrate his varied talents on some other subject. A fat insurance policy, of course, followed by a well-organized fire, would have been more profitable; but a recent sensational arson trial and the consequent publicity given to such schemes made him wary of taking that way out. And he

156

was engrossed in these uninspiring meditations when the bell in his "office" rang and manna fell from Heaven.

Mr. Oscar Newdick, it must be acknowledged, did not instantly recognize it as manna. At first he thought it could only be the rate collector, or another summons for his unpaid electric light bill. He tiptoed to a grimy window which looked out on the road, with intent to escape rapidly across the adjacent fields if his surmise proved correct; and it was thus that he saw the imposing automobile which stood outside.

Mr. Newdick, a man of the world, was jerry to the fact that rate collectors and servers of summonses rarely arrive to their grim work in five-thousand-pound Hirondels; and it was with an easy conscience, if not yet admixed with undue optimism, that he went to open the door.

"Hullo, old bean," said the Saint.

"Er—hullo," said Mr. Newdick.

"I blew in to see if you could tell me anything about your jolly old company," said the Saint.

"Er—yes," said Mr. Newdick. "Er—why don't you come inside?"

His hesitation was not due to any bashfulness or even to offended dignity. Mr. Newdick did not mind being called an old bean. He had no instinctive desire to snub wealthy-looking young men with five-thousand-pound Hirondels who added jollity to his old company. The fact was that he was just beginning to recognize the manna for what it was, and his soul was suffering the same emotions as those which had afflicted the Israelites in their time when they contemplated the miracle.

The Saint came in. Mr. Newdick's "office" was a small roughly fashioned cubicle about the size of a telephone booth, containing a small table littered with papers and overlaid with a thin film of dust—it scarcely seemed in keeping with the neatly engraved brass plate on the door which proclaimed it to be the registered offices of the Newdick Helicopter Company, Limited, but his visitor did not seem distressed by it.

"What did you want to know?" asked Mr. Newdick.

Simon observed him to be a middle-aged man of only vaguely military appearance, with sharp eyes that looked at him unwaveringly. That characteristic alone might have deceived most men; but Simon Templar had moved in disreputable circles long enough to know that the ability to look another man squarely in the eye is one of the most fallacious indices of honesty.

"Well," said the Saint amiably, tendering a platinum cigarette case, "the fact is that I'm interested in helicopters. I happen to have noticed your little place several times recently when I've been passing, and I got the idea that it was quite a small show, and I wondered if there might by any chance be room for another partner in it."

"You mean," repeated Mr. Newdick, checking back on the incredible evidence of his ears, "that you wanted to take an interest in the firm?"

Simon nodded.

"That was the jolly old idea," he said. "In fact, if the other partners felt like selling out, I might take over the whole blinkin' show. I've got a good deal of time on my hands, and I like pottering about with airplanes and whatnot. A chap's got to do something to keep out of mischief, what? Besides, it doesn't look as if you were doing a lot of business here, and I might be able to wake the jolly old place up a bit. Sort of aerial roadhouse, if you know what I mean. Dinners—drinks—dancing—pretty girls . . . What?"

"I didn't say anything," said Mr. Newdick.

"All right. What about it, old bean?"

Mr. Newdick scratched his chin. The notion of manna had passed into his cosmogony. It fell from Heaven. It was real. Miracles happened. The world was a brighter, rosier place.

"One of your remarks, of course," he said, "is somewhat uninformed. As a matter of fact, we are doing quite a lot of business. We have orders, negotiations, tenders, contracts . . . ." The eloquent movement of one hand, temporarily released from massaging his chin, indicated a whole field of industry of which the uninitiated were in ignorance. "However," he said, "if your proposition were attractive enough, it would be worth hearing."

Simon nodded.

"Well, old bean, who do I put it to?"

"You may put it to me, if you like," said Mr. Newdick. "I am Oscar Newdick."

"I see. But what about the other partners, Oscar, old sprout?"

Mr. Newdick waved his hand.

"They are largely figureheads," he explained. "A few friends, with very small interests—just enough to meet the technical requirements of a limited company. The concern really belongs to me."

Simon beamed.

"Splendid!" he said. "Jolly good! Well, well, well, dear old Newdick, what d'you think it's worth?"

"There is a nominal share value of twenty-five thousand pounds," said Mr. Newdick seriously. "But, of course, they are worth far more than that. Far more. . . . I very much doubt," he said, "whether fifty thousand would be an adequate price. My patents alone are worth more than fifty thousand pounds. Sixty thousand pounds would scarcely tempt me. Seventy thousand would be a poor price. Eighty thousand—"

"It's quite a lot of money," said the Saint, interrupting Mr. Newdick's private auction.

Mr. Newdick nodded.

"But you haven't seen the place yet—or the machine we turn out. You ought to have a look around, even if we can't do business."

Mr. Newdick suffered a twinge of horror at the thought even while he uttered it.

He led the Saint out of his "office" to the junk shed. No one who had witnessed his sad survey of that collection of lumber a few minutes before would have believed that it was the same man who now gazed on it with such enthusiasm and affection.

"This," said Mr. Newdick, "is our workshop. Here you can

see the parts of our machines in course of construction and assembly. Those lengths of wood are our special longerons. Over there are stays and braces . . ."

"By Jove!" said the Saint in awe. "I'd no idea helicopters went in for all those things. They must be quite dressed up when you've finished them, what? By the way, talking of longerons, a girlfriend of mine has the neatest pattern of step-ins . . ."

Mr. Newdick listened patiently.

Presently they passed on to the other shed. Mr. Newdick opened the doors as reverently as if he had been unveiling a memorial.

"And this," he said, "is the Newdick helicopter."

Simon glanced over it vacuously, and looked about him.

"Where are all your workmen today?" he asked.

"They are on holiday," said Mr. Newdick, making a mental note to engage some picturesque mechanics the next day. "An old custom of the firm. I always give them a full day's holiday on the anniversary of my dear mother's death." He wiped away a tear and changed the subject. "How would you like to take a flight?"

"Jolly good idea," agreed the Saint.

The helicopter was wheeled out, and while it was warming up, Simon revealed that he also was a flier and possessed a license for helicopters. Mr. Newdick complimented him gravely. They made a ten-minute flight, and when they had landed again the Saint remained in his seat.

"D'you mind if I try her out myself?" he said. "I won't ask you to take the flight with me."

The machine was not fitted with dual control, but it was well insured. Mr. Newdick only hesitated a moment. He was very anxious to please.

"Certainly," he said. "Give her a thorough test yourself, and you'll see that she's a good bus."

Simon took the ship off and climbed toward the north. When Mr. Newdick's tiny aerodrome was out of sight he put the helicopter through every test he could think of, and the

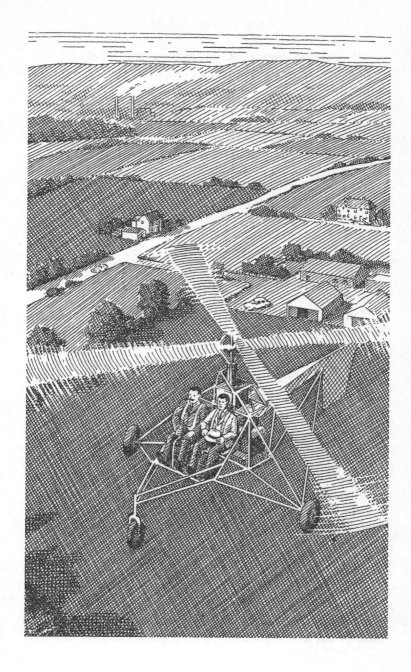

results amazed him even while they only confirmed the remarkable impression he had gained while Mr. Newdick was flying it.

When he saw the London Air Park below him he shut off the engine and came down in a perfect vertical descent which set him down outside the Cierva hangars. Simon climbed out and buttonholed one of the company's test pilots.

"Would you like to come on a short hop with me?" he asked. "I want to show you something."

As they walked back toward the Newdick helicopter the pilot studied it with a puzzled frown.

"Is that one of our machines?" he said.

"More or less," Simon told him.

"It looks as if it had been put together wrong," said the pilot worriedly. "Have you been having trouble with it?"

The Saint shook his head.

"I think you'll find," he answered, "that it's been put together right."

He demonstrated what he meant, and when they returned the test pilot took the machine up again himself and tried it a second time. Other test pilots tried it. Engineers scratched their heads over it and tried it. Telephone calls were made to London. A whole two hours passed before Simon Templar dropped the machine beside Mr. Newdick's sheds and relieved the inventor of the agonies of anxiety which had been racking him.

"I was afraid you'd killed yourself," said Mr. Newdick with emotion; and indeed the thought that his miraculous benefactor might have passed away before being separated from his money had brought Mr. Newdick out in several cold sweats.

The Saint grinned.

"I just buzzed over to Reading to look up a friend," he said untruthfully. "I like your helicopter. Let us go inside and talk business."

When he returned to Patricia, much later that day, he was jubilant but mysterious. He spent most of the next day with

162

Mr. Newdick, and half of the Saturday which came after, but he refused to tell her what he was doing. It was not until that evening, when he was pouring beer once more for Monty Hayward, that he mentioned Mr. Newdick again; and then his announcement took her breath away.

"I've bought that helicopter company," he said casually.

"You've what?" spluttered Monty.

"I've bought that helicopter company and everything it owns," said the Saint, "for forty thousand pounds."

They gaped at him for a while in silence, while he calmly continued with the essential task of opening bottles.

"The man's mad," said Patricia finally. "I always thought so."

"When did you do this?" asked Monty.

"We fixed up the last details of the deal today," said the Saint. "Oscar is due here at any minute to sign the papers."

Monty swallowed beer feverishly.

"I suppose you wouldn't care to buy my shares as well?" he suggested.

"Sure, I'll buy them," said the Saint affably. "Name your price. Oscar's contribution gives me a controlling interest, but I can always handle a bit more. As ordered by Patricia, I'm going into business. The machine is to be rechristened the Templar helicopter. I shall go down in history as the man who put England in the air. Bevies of English beauty, wearing their Templar longerons—stays, braces, and everything complete—"

The ringing of his doorbell interrupted the word-picture and took him from the room before any of the questions that were howling through their bewildered minds could be asked.

Mr. Newdick was on the mat, beaming like a delighted fox. Simon took his hat and umbrella, took Mr. Newdick by the arm, and led him through into the living room.

"Boys and girls," he said cheerfully, "this is our fairy godmother, Mr. Oscar Newdick. This is Miss Holm, Oscar, old toadstool; and I think you know Mr. Hayward—"

The inventor's arm had stiffened under his hand, and his smile had vanished. His face was turning pale and nasty.

"What's the game?" he demanded hoarsely.

"No game at all, dear old garlic-blossom," said the Saint innocently. "Just a coincidence. Mr. Hayward is going to sell me his shares, too. Now, all the papers are here, and if you'll just sign on the dotted line—"

"I refuse!" babbled Newdick wildly. "It's a trap!"

Simon stepped back and regarded him blandly.

"A trap, Oscar? What on earth are you talking about? You've got a jolly good helicopter, and you've nothing to be ashamed of. Come, now, be brave. Harden the Newdick heart. There may be a wrench at parting with your brainchild, but you can cry afterwards. Just a signature or two on the dotted line, and it's all over. And there's a check for forty thousand pounds waiting for you . . . ."

He thrust a fountain pen into the inventor's hand; and, half-hypnotized, Mr. Newdick signed. The Saint blotted the signatures carefully and put the agreements away in a drawer, which he locked. Then he handed Mr. Newdick a check. The inventor grasped it weakly and stared at the writing and figures on it as if he expected them to fade away under his eyes. He had the quite natural conviction that his brain had given way.

"Th-thank you very much," he said shakily, and was conscious of little more than an overpowering desire to remove himself from those parts—to camp out on the doorstep of a bank and wait there with his head in his hands until morning, when he could pass the check over the counter and see crisp banknotes clicking back to him in return to prove that his sanity was not entirely gone. "Well, I must be going," he gulped out; but the Saint stopped him.

"Not a bit of it, Oscar," he murmured. "You don't intrude. In fact, you ought to be the guest of honor. Your class as an inventor really is A1. When I showed the Cierva people what you'd done, they nearly collapsed."

Mr. Newdick blinked at him in a painful daze.

"What do you mean?" he stammered.

"Why, the way you managed to build an autogiro that would go straight up and down. None of the ordinary ones will, of course—the torque of the vanes would make it spin around like a top if it didn't have a certain amount of forward movement to hold it straight. I can only think that when you got hold of some Cierva parts and drawings and built it up yourself, you found out that it didn't go straight up and down as you'd expected and thought you must have done something wrong. So you set about trying to put it right—and somehow or other you brought it off. It's a pity you were in such a hurry to tell Mr. Hayward that everything in your invention had been patented before, Oscar, because if you'd made a few more inquiries you'd have found that it hadn't." Simon Templar grinned, and patted the stunned man kindly on the shoulder. "But everything happens for the best, dear old bird; and when I tell you that the Cierva people have already made me an offer of a hundred thousand quid for the invention you've just sold me, I'm sure you'll stay and join us in a celebratory bottle of beer."

Mr. Oscar Newdick swayed slightly, and glugged a strangling obstruction out of his throat.

"I—I don't think I'll stay," he said. "I'm not feeling very well."

"A dose of salts in the morning will do you all the good in the world," said the Saint chattily, and ushered him sympathetically to the door.

MORE FROM THE FILES OF INSPECTOR CRAIG

RAYMOND SMULLYAN

Sometimes Inspector Craig would exercise his logical mind on mysteries he didn't personally investigate. Here are some puzzles he came across while visiting the Law Courts.

1

A man was being tried for participation in a robbery. The prosecutor and the defense attorney made the following statements:

Prosecutor
If the defendant is guilty, then he had an accomplice.

Defense Attorney
That's not true!

Why was this the worst thing the defense attorney could have said?

2

This and the next case involve the trial of three men A, B, C for participation in a robbery.

In this case, the following two facts were established:

(1) If A is innocent or B is guilty, then C is guilty.
(2) If A is innocent, then C is innocent.

Can the guilt of any particular one of the three be established?

3

In this case, the following facts were established:

(1) At least one of the three is guilty.
(2) If A is guilty and B is innocent, then C is guilty.

This evidence is insufficient to convict any of them, but it does point to two of them such that one of these two has to be guilty. Which two are they?

4

In this more interesting case, four defendants A, B, C, D were involved and the following four facts were established:

(1) If both A and B are guilty, then C was an accomplice.
(2) If A is guilty, then at least one of B, C was an accomplice.
(3) If C is guilty, then D was an accomplice.
(4) If A is innocent then D is guilty.

Which ones are definitely guilty and which ones are doubtful?

For Inspector Craig's solutions see page 221.

THE ONE-HANDED MURDERER

ITALO CALVINO

An Italian folktale

Most folktales aren't murder stories, but this one is. There are no fairies in this tale—nothing supernatural at all; just crime and vengeance. But it's more vivid and suspenseful than many a ghost story. The murderer who pursues the princess from one country to another is like a figure from a nightmare, and only the princess can save herself; everyone else is asleep . . .

THERE WAS ONCE a miser king, so miserly that he kept his only daughter in the garret for fear someone would ask for her hand and thus oblige him to provide her with a dowry.

One day a murderer came to town and stopped at the inn across the street from the king's palace. Right away he wanted to know who lived over there. "That's the home of a king," he was told, "so miserly that he keeps his daughter in the garret."

So what does the murderer do at night but climb up on the king's roof and open the small garret window. Lying in bed, the princess saw the window open and a man on the ledge.

"Help! Burglar!" she screamed. The murderer closed the window and fled over the rooftops. The servants came running, saw the window closed, and said, "Your Highness, you were dreaming. There's no one here."

The next morning she asked her father to let her out of the garret, but the king said, "Your fears are imaginary. No one in the world would ever think of coming up here."

The second night the murderer opened the window at the same hour. "Help! Burglar!" screamed the princess, but again he got away, and no one would believe her.

The third night she fastened the window with a strong chain and, with pounding heart, stood guard all by herself holding a knife. The murderer tried to open the window, but couldn't. He thrust in one hand, and the princess cut it clean off at the wrist. "You wretch!" cried the murderer. "You'll pay for that!" And he fled over the rooftops.

The princess showed the king and the court the amputated hand, and everybody finally believed her and complimented her courage. From that day on, she no longer slept in the garret.

Not too long after that, the king received a request for an audience from an elegant young stranger who wore gloves. He was so well-spoken that the king took an instant liking to him. Talking of this and that, the stranger mentioned that he was a bachelor in search of a genteel bride, whom he would marry without a dowry, being so wealthy himself. Hearing that, the king thought, This is just the husband for my daughter, and he sent for her. The minute the princess saw the man she shuddered, having the strong impression she already knew him. Once she was alone with her father, she said, "Majesty, I'm all but sure that's the burglar whose hand I cut off."

"Nonsense," replied the king. "Didn't you notice his beautiful hands and elegant gloves? He's a nobleman beyond any shadow of a doubt."

To make a long story short, the stranger asked for the princess's hand, and to obey her father and escape his tyranny, she said yes. The wedding was short and simple, since the bridegroom couldn't remain away from his business and the king was unwilling to spend any money. He gave his daughter, for a bridal present, a walnut necklace and a worn-out foxtail. Then the newlyweds drove off at once in a carriage.

The carriage entered a forest, but instead of following the main road it turned off on to a scarcely visible trail that led deeper and deeper into the underbrush. When they had gone some distance, the bridegroom said, "My dear, pull off my glove."

She did, and discovered a stump. "Help!" she cried, realizing she'd married the man whose hand she had cut off.

"You're in my power now," said the man. "I am a murderer by profession, mind you. I'll now get even with you for maiming me."

The murderer's house was at the edge of the forest, by the sea. "Here I've stored all the treasure of my victims," he said, pointing to the house, "and you will stay and guard it."

He chained her to a tree in front of the house and walked off. The princess remained by herself, tethered like a dog, and before her was the sea, over which a ship glided from time to time. She tried signaling to a passing ship. On board they saw her through their telescope and sailed closer to see what the matter was. The crew disembarked, and she told them her story. So they set her free and took her aboard, together with all the murderer's treasure.

It was a ship of cotton merchants, who thought it wise to conceal the princess and all the treasure underneath the bales of cotton. The murderer returned and found his wife gone and the house ransacked. She could have only escaped by the sea, he thought to himself, and then saw the ship disappearing into the distance. He got into his swift sailing boat and caught up with the ship. "All that cotton overboard!" he ordered. "I must find my wife who has fled."

"Do you want to ruin us?" asked the merchants. "Why not run your sword through the bales to see if anyone is hiding in them?"

The murderer started piercing the cotton with his sword and, before long, wounded the girl hiding there. But as he drew his sword out, the cotton wiped the blood off, and the sword came out clean.

"Listen," said the sailors, "we saw another ship approach the coast, that one down there."

"I'll investigate at once," said the murderer. He left the ship carrying cotton and directed his sailing boat toward the other ship.

The girl, who had received a mere scratch on her arm, was put ashore in a safe port. But she protested, saying, "Throw me into the sea! Throw me into the sea!"

The sailors talked the matter over, and one old-timer in their midst, whose wife had no children, offered to take the girl home with him, together with part of the murderer's jewels. The sailor's wife was a good old soul and gave her a mother's love. "Poor dear, you will be our daughter!"

"You are such good people," said the girl. "I'm going to ask just one favor: let me always stay inside and be seen by no man."

"Don't worry, dear, nobody ever comes to our house."

The old man sold a few jewels and bought embroidery silk, so the girl spent her time embroidering. She made an exquisite tablecloth, working into it every color and design under the sun, and the old woman took it to the nearby house of a king to sell.

"But who does this fine work?" asked the king.

"One of my daughters, Majesty," replied the old woman.

"Go on! That doesn't look like the work of a sailor's daughter," said the king, and bought the tablecloth.

The old woman used the money to buy more silk, and the girl embroidered a beautiful folding screen, which the old woman also took to the king.

"Is this really your daughter's work?" asked the king. He was still suspicious, and secretly followed her home.

Just as the old woman was closing the door, the king walked up and stuck his foot in it; the old woman let out a cry.

Hearing the cry from her room, the girl thought the murderer had come after her and she fainted from fright. The old woman and the king came in and tried to revive her. She opened her eyes and, seeing that it was not the murderer, regained her senses.

"But what are you so afraid of?" asked the king, charmed with this girl.

"It's just my bad luck," she replied, and would say nothing more.

So the king started going to that house every day to keep the girl company and watch her embroider. He had fallen in love with her and finally asked for her hand in marriage. You can just imagine the old people's amazement. "Majesty, we are poor people," they began.

"No matter, I'm interested in the girl."

"I am willing," said the maiden, "but on one condition."

"What is that?"

"I refuse to see all men regardless of who they are, except you and my father." (She now called the old sailor her father.) "I will neither see them nor be seen by them."

The king consented to that. Jealous beyond measure, he was delighted she wanted to see no man but him.

Thus were they married in secret, so that no man would see her. The king's subjects were not at all happy over the matter, for when had a king ever married without showing the people his wife? The strangest of rumors began circulating. "He's married a monkey. He's married a hunchback. He's married a witch." Nor were the people the only ones to gossip; the highest dignitaries at the court also talked. So the king was forced to say to his wife, "You must appear in public for one hour and put an end to all those rumors."

The poor thing had no choice but to obey. "Very well, tomorrow morning from eleven till noon I will appear on the terrace."

At eleven o'clock, the square was more packed than it had ever been. People had come from all over the country, even from the backwoods. The bride walked onto the terrace, and a murmur of admiration went up from the crowd. Never had they seen so beautiful a queen. She, however, scanned the crowd with uneasiness, and there in its midst stood a man cloaked in black. He brought his hand to his mouth and bit it in a threatening gesture, then held up his other arm, which ended in a stump. The queen sank to the ground in a swoon.

They carried her inside at once, and the old woman said over and over, "You would have to show her off! You would have to show her off against her will. Now just see what's happened!"

The queen was put to bed, and all the doctors were called in, but her illness baffled everyone. She insisted on remaining shut up and seeing no one, and she trembled all the time.

Meanwhile the king received a visit from a well-to-do foreign gentleman with a glib tongue and full of flattery. The king invited him to stay for dinner. The stranger, who was none other than the murderer, graciously accepted and ordered wine for everyone in the royal palace. Casks, barrels, and demijohns were brought in at once, but every drop of the wine had been drugged. That evening, guards, servants, ministers, and everybody else drank their fill and, by night, they were dead drunk and snoring, the king loudest of all.

The murderer went through the palace making sure that on the stairs, in the corridors and all the rooms there was no one who wasn't flat on his back and sleeping. Then he tiptoed into the queen's room and found her hunched up in a corner of her bed and wide-eyed, almost as though she expected him.

"The hour has come for my revenge," hissed the murderer. "Get out of bed and fetch me a basin of water to wash the blood from my hands when I've cut your throat."

The queen ran out of the room to her husband. "Wake up! For heaven's sake, wake up!" But he slept on. Everybody in the whole palace slept, and there was no way in the world to wake them up. She got the basin of water and returned to her room.

"Bring me some soap, too," ordered the murderer as he sharpened his knife.

She went out, tried once more to rouse her husband, but to no avail. She then returned with the soap.

"And the towel?" asked the murderer.

She went out, got the pistol off her sleeping husband, wrapped it in the towel and, making a motion to hand the towel to the murderer, fired a shot point-blank into his heart.

At that shot, the drunk people all woke up at the same time and, with the king in the lead, ran into her room. They found the murderer slain and the queen freed at last from her terror.

THE LITTLE MYSTERY

E. C. BENTLEY

This comes from the age of the classic English detective story, when rich and fashionable people seemed to discover a body in their country house library every week, and only the sharp-eyed amateur detective was able to solve the mystery. Scotland Yard, of course, was permanently baffled.

There were not very many stories about Philip Trent, but he was one of the most sharp-eyed of all. In this story he sees at once the significance of the four little scratches on the tabletop. And despite what Marion Silvester thinks, it does turn out to be a crime problem after all.

It was early on a Saturday afternoon that Philip Trent, passing through Cadogan Place, caught sight of a trim figure in the portico of one of the tall old houses. The girl came down the steps as he stopped his car.

"How goes it, Marion?" he said. "It must be all of a year since I saw you last."

"Why, Phil! What a surprise!" She glanced back at the door she had just left. "Have you come to see the doctor? But no, you can't do that without an appointment—and besides, he's just going out himself."

Trent got out of the driving seat and shook hands with Marion Silvester, whom he had known for most of her twenty-two years. "So this is the doctor's. Ah yes, I see—brass plate so tiny you don't notice it's there. A great man, evidently —the smaller the plate the bigger the doctor. Still, I don't want to see him. I have just been lunching in Chelsea, but it wasn't as bad as all that."

"Well, you will see him, whether you want to or not," she said in a low tone as the door opened, and a tall, gaunt man, black-bearded, came out. He took off his hat to Marion, with a swift glance at Trent as he returned the salutation, and passed on his way.

"He's not a doctor, really, he's a surgeon," Marion explained. "But he is a Pole, and it seems that whatever degree you take in his country, you're called a doctor."

Trent examined the brass plate. "Dr. W. Kozicki. There is something very tragic about the look of your Dr. W. Kozicki, Marion. An interesting, cultured face. And he has very small ears, with hardly any lobes. Beautiful hands; and he has had the left one badly bitten by a dog, or possibly a patient—some years ago by the look of the scar. No baldness, though he must be over fifty. Short nose, long upper lip—he wouldn't look nearly so handsome if he was clean-shaved."

She laughed. "Isn't that just like you! You see a person for a split second, and you've got him photographed. Well, I'm his secretary, and as Saturday's a short day, I get off after lunch."

"Is there anywhere I can take you? I am free for the next hour."

She thought for a moment. "You know, Phil, meeting you like this is really rather lucky. Several times I've wished I could tell you about something that's been annoying me, because I can't understand it, and perhaps you could, though it's not one of your crime problems. If you could take me home, I could explain it best there. I suppose you don't know Reville Place."

"I know where it is."

"Then you know it's where a quite nice neighborhood shades off into a dingy one. I've got a cheap top floor at number 43." Trent opened the door of the car, and she took her place. "It's not a very cheery spot, but my flatlet is all right once you're inside the door. Mother let me have some decent furniture and things, and it's airy and comfortable."

The car started, and Marion continued, "Yes, I am on my own now. Of course, we haven't met since Father died. We weren't left any too well off, as you may imagine, knowing him as you did."

Trent nodded. He had indeed known Colin Silvester well enough to be surprised that he had left anything at all. Probably, he reflected, Mrs. Silvester had her own income. Silvester had made money easily and abundantly, but he had loved entertaining on a generous scale, and loved yet more anything in the nature of a gamble for high stakes. He had been well known and popular in the social world, though a malicious wit had made him not everyone's friend; which had added a spice to the news that, at his death, he had left behind him the material for a volume of memoirs, to be published in due time.

"Mother has the house in Wallingford," Marion said, "and not too much to run it on, when Fred's school bills have been paid. I had a little capital of my own, enough to keep me while I was learning to make a living, so I decided to come to London and train for a secretary's job. I took this place we're going to, and started a course at Needham's."

Trent asked when she had finished her course.

"Why, I never did finish it," Marion said. "I hadn't been at it three months when Paula Kozicki looked me up. You wouldn't know her—she's my boss's daughter, of course, and she was my greatest friend at school. She had all her education in England, and you would never know she was a Pole. She's lived with her father since he came to London. He had a son who went to the devil, Paula told me, and since then the old man has been entirely devoted to her. Well, when she called on me, she told me her father wanted a new secretary, and nothing would do but that he must have me for the job.

"I was astonished. I had only seen him once in my life, when Paula brought him to tea in Reville Place. I had heard about him sometimes from Father, who for some reason didn't like him, and I had always imagined he was very disagreeable; but when he came I quite took to the old chap, he so evidently doted on Paula. But of course I hadn't ever dreamed of an offer like this. Well, she made me come round and see him; and he was most charming—said he had been so much touched by Paula's story of me and my doings—he laid it on rather thick, really. You know the sort of thing men say when a girl doesn't merely curl up and collapse when things get difficult."

"Yes, I do know," Trent said with feeling. "Your pluck, your self-reliance, your—"

"All right, I see you've got it by heart," interrupted the girl of the period. "So when we had got over that part, he asked if I could come to him, as his secretary was leaving him for a better position—which I knew from Paula; only she also told me the doctor had got her another post because he wanted to have me. I said how gratified I was, but that I had had very little training and no experience; and he said any fool could do the work—though he didn't put it quite that way—as it was just keeping a list of appointments with patients, and receiving them when they came, and taking some correspondence, and noting up the fees. And then he offered me about double what I should have expected for my first job.

"Well, I took it. There was absolutely nothing wrong with it; and there still isn't, after a month of it. The work's not hard, and in fact there's often not much to do, so that I can get a little work done on Father's book. Oh! I didn't tell you that I was putting his rough notes for his memoirs into shape for the publishers. They're very rough ones, and I have to write the whole thing out myself. I take some of the stuff to the doctor's every day. There's quite a lot of it—I haven't read it all yet, in fact; but a good deal of what I have read is pretty scandalous, believe me."

Trent, with a vivid memory of Silvester's vein of unexpurgated anecdote about people of importance, said that this was easy to believe. "But you say there's still nothing wrong with this heaven-sent job of yours. Marion, you blast my hopes. I thought I was going to hear that Kozicki had made dishonorable proposals to you, or that he drinks laudanum, or that he has a private delusion that he is a weasel. Well, it's all very capital for you, and I am gladder than I can say—and here we are at 43 Reville Place."

This was an old-fashioned, high-roofed, stucco-fronted house with a basement and three other floors; like all its neighbors, slightly dingy in appearance, though not dilapidated. They mounted the steps, and Marion opened the door with a latchkey. It could be seen, as they went up the stairs, that each floor had been partitioned off to form a self-contained flat; and Marion's own door, like the front door, was fitted with a Yale lock.

"Well, here's my top floor," she said as they entered. There were four rooms opening off the landing, all fairly lofty and well lighted.

"And a very good top floor," Trent observed when he had been shown the living room, bedroom, bathroom, and kitchen. "Much better than the top floor in my own place; and furnished, as I think you said, with faultless taste. If ever you want to get rid of that little tallboy you might let me know. And that mahogany writing table—it was a spinet when it was young, wasn't it? You want to keep that, I suppose."

Marion laughed. "Are you setting up an antique shop? But now, let me tell you what it was I wanted your advice about. To begin with, look at the top of that table."

He bent over it. "You mean these faint scratches here and there—as if something hard and heavy had been shifted about on it. Curious? The scratches are in four lots—making the four corners of a square. Was it done when the furniture was moved here from Wallingford?"

"No, it was done fairly lately—three weeks ago, say; perhaps more. That table was as smooth as glass till then. I rub it over with a duster every day, so I noticed it at once. And it wasn't done by the charlady who comes in two mornings a week. She is a very careful, neat-handed woman; and besides,

I first saw the scratches on a Thursday, and her days are Tuesday and Friday. Of course, I don't like having my table scratched, but what I like much less is not knowing who did it, and how anyone could have been here to do it. The entrance door is locked when I'm out, of course; and the street door always is. And don't look as if you thought I was worrying about a trifle. There are other things that tell me plainly someone comes into this place when I'm not here.

"You see the velvet cushion in that armchair? It's embroidered a prettier pattern on one side than on the other, and I always leave it showing that side, as it is now. But several times I have come in and found it turned the other way round. Anyone who had been sitting in that chair, and had punched the cushion into shape again before going away, would be as likely as not to leave it the wrong way round. Then again there is that old writing table you covet so much. There is nothing of value in either of the drawers—I keep Father's notes for his memoirs in the left-hand one, and as much as I have done of the fair copy in the other—but three times someone has been at them."

"They are not locked?" Trent asked.

"No—nothing in the place is locked except the door of the flat. Now, look at these drawers. You see,"—she opened both and shut them again—"they both push in a little too far when you close them, and I always pull them back so as to be just level with the woodwork round them. I'm fussily particular, perhaps you think; anyhow, I am absolutely certain I have never left those drawers pushed right in as I found them three days running not long ago. And now here,"—she led the way into the kitchen—"I'll show you the thing that makes me quite certain, and that is this sink. When I've washed up after breakfast I leave it not only perfectly clean, but quite dry, bottom and sides as well."

"Why?" Trent wondered.

"Because I've been well brought up," Marion said conclusively. "Well, every day for some time past I have come home and found it perfectly clean, but not dry—drops of water on the sides, which you get from the splashes when you're running the tap. Look! You see those drops? A man wouldn't, I suppose, unless they were pointed out to him. They weren't here when I left this morning."

Marion and her guest looked at one another in silence for some moments; then Trent remarked, "You say nothing about having missed anything—jewelry, or any other sort of portable property."

"No," she said. "Absolutely nothing has ever been stolen, I am sure. I often leave money in my dressing table drawer, and my jewelry, such as it is, is kept there, too, and nothing has been taken. What food I have had in the place has never been touched, nor any of the household things—unless you count those matches, which I suppose came from my box."

Trent rose and paced the floor. "It all sounds pretty mad, I must say," he observed. "And it doesn't make it seem any saner to suggest that one of the people on the lower floors may be your visitor, as they haven't got your private key."

"Yes, and besides, why should they? As for my keys, they are always in my handbag, which is with me all the time. The only duplicates are a pair I keep in the dressing table drawer, and a pair the charwoman has; and if you ever saw Mrs. Kinch you would know she was incapable of doing anything eccentric or not respectable. She worships the Vicar of St. Mark's, just round the corner, and she sings hymns while she is doing out the place, as she calls it; and she has a son in a lawyer's office, and likes to let you know it. There have been other things, too, which you can't possibly connect with Mrs. Kinch. There's that window you saw me shut when we came in. She knows I always leave it open, to air the room. Well, several times I have come home and found it shut. You see?"

Trent went to the window and opened it for a moment. "Yes, there might be a draft that anyone sitting in this armchair would feel. I agree; it does look as if somebody has been coming in here while you were away—in particular, sitting in your armchair, and plumping up the cushion when he leaves the place."

An exclamation of disgust came from Marion Silvester. "And that's a nice thing to think of, isn't it? I prefer to know something about people who visit my flat and sprawl in my armchair. And it's no use going to the police about it, as you can see. What have I got to tell them? The place hasn't been broken into, nothing has been stolen. I've no actual proof that anyone has been making themselves at home here. They'd only grin, and say—or think—I was far ¬ying things."

Trent considered. "Yes, I suppose they would. By the way, what time do you leave here in the morning?"

"Nine-fifteen; and get back about seven, usually."

"Much at home during the weekends?"

"No, not a lot. I spend a good deal of the time with friends —Paula Kozicki and other people I know in London. On Sundays I get out into the country if the weather's decent, and have a day in the open air, with or without a companion. I don't have at all a dull life, Phil. The one bad spot is this silly little mystery."

"Perhaps," Trent said, "the best thing you can do, Marion, is to leave it to me. I must be on my way now, but I will let my giant intellect play round the subject, and make a few inquiries and see you again very soon."

She jumped up. "Heaven bless you, Phil! That's what I hoped you would say."

"And before I go, would you like to trust me with those spare keys of yours?"

She fetched them from the bedroom. "If you use them, you must promise not to pilfer anything, or smash up the furniture."

Trent expressed the hope that he would be able to overcome his lower nature. Before he left the house, he tried each of the keys in its lock, and found that they fitted easily.

In the Cactus Club, most ways of life are represented, and there are few subjects on which some information cannot be gleaned from fellow members whenever there is a large muster. Lunching there the next day, Trent was able to draw upon more than one source for facts about Dr. Kozicki. He was an orthopedic specialist with certain methods of his own devising and a fancy for making his own surgical appliances. He had built up a large practice in his native city of Posen, and made a European reputation. The afflicted grandson of Jason B. Rhodes, the sulphur magnate, had been brought across the ocean to him for treatment, and had been cured.

An ex-patient of the doctor, who had attended him at his own house, gave some more intimate details. Kozicki was a widower. His son and daughter had been sent to school in England, so as to escape the influence of German culture, of which the doctor disapproved, for he had been an ardent Polish patriot under the German rule. This had not been a success in the case of the son, who had turned out a hopeless waster.

Some ten years ago Dr. Kozicki had, it was vaguely known, "got into trouble" with the German authorities, and had found it advisable to transfer himself to London, where he had resumed his practice, and was doing more than well. The son, going from bad to worse, had turned his attention to forgery, and had been sent to penal servitude. The doctor was entirely wrapped up in his daughter, who was a Slade art student. He had not succeeded in spoiling her, and everyone thought her charming.

Beside his liking for Marion Silvester, Trent had another motive for taking up her "little mystery." He thought there might be something more to the affair than she imagined, and his curiosity was awake. It might be worthwhile to look further into the affairs of Dr. Kozicki; and there was one line, at least, that could be followed up. After leaving the Cactus Club, he spent a fruitless hour searching the files in the offices of the *Record* for a report of the trial of the younger Kozicki; and he was still at this task when Homan, the paper's regular crime expert, came into the library.

"If you're hunting for the name Kozicki," Homan said, "you won't find it. I remember the case. He was prosecuted under the name of Jackson, by which he was known to the police as being mixed up with a bad lot. He had forged a stolen check and collected the money. It didn't come out till afterwards that he was the doctor's son, and the fact was never made public. He was informed on by a man he had quarreled with, and his evidence got Jackson five years."

Thus put on the right track, Trent soon turned up the report of the case. It was colorless enough; but Trent noted that the name of the informer was given as Whimster, that he had been on intimate terms with Jackson before their quarrel, and that his going to the police had the air of an act of treachery rather than of dauntless public spirit. A public house called the Cat and Fiddle, in the Harrow Road, had figured in the evidence as a rendezvous of Jackson, Whimster, and their associates. A comparison of dates showed that Jackson-Kozicki's sentence still had six months to run; but as Homan pointed out, it might be shortened considerably as the reward for good conduct.

The landlord of the Cat and Fiddle, whose beer Trent found to be in excellent condition, had known Whimster very well. Jackson had been before his time. When the landlord first came to the place, three years ago, Whimster had been using the Cat and Fiddle regularly. He was a racing tipster, and seemed to do pretty well out of it, taking good times with bad. Last year Whimster had left the district, saying nothing to nobody; but Joe Chittle, being over in Woolwich not long ago, had seen him in the street. Joe could swear it was Whimster; but when he spoke to him he said that wasn't his name, and he had never seen Joe in his life—quite nasty about it he was, Joe said. Well, what could you make of it?

Funny, but Trent was not the first to be asking after Whimster, the landlord said. There had been a gent in not long ago wanting to get in touch with the same party, and the landlord had told him the same as he had told Trent.

"Would you know that man again?" asked Trent.

Yes, the landlord would; it was a face that gave you a funny feeling, you couldn't easily forget it. But what, the landlord wondered, was the reason for all this interest in Whimster?

Trent could only tell him that he thought Whimster might have some information that would be useful to him. What was the landlord having? The landlord's was a toothful of old Jamaica—good stuff this chilly weather. Happy days, sir!

Chief Inspector Bligh, receiving Trent in his little office at Scotland Yard, pushed the cigarette box across the table.

"Yes, I can tell you something more about Ladislas Kozicki, alias George Jackson," Mr Bligh said, when Trent had set forth the extent of his own information. "I'm glad you got the landlord of the Cat to talk; his evidence will be useful. We hadn't got on to that line, because, you see, the man you know as Whimster has called himself Barling since he went to live in Woolwich. They must be the same man; I can see that. We have got plenty on Jackson as it is, but you can't have too much."

"Why, is he in trouble again?"

"You might call it that," the inspector said grimly. "He came out of prison five weeks ago. He's wanted now for attempted murder. Last Tuesday night, Barling passed two men who knew him walking up Foxhill Street, where he lives. There was nobody else about. They exchanged greetings as they passed; and then the two chaps met another, whose face they say they didn't like. This fellow was staring after Barling, and looked as if he was following him. Well, out of curiosity they turned and followed, too.

"Just as Barling was approaching a pub called the Red Cow, which he was probably on his way to, they saw the follower catch him up and take him by the arm. They were too far behind to hear what was said, but the other man seemed to steer Barling into the entry of a builder's yard at the side of the pub. Then they heard Barling yelling for help, and as they ran up, the other man came bolting out of the entry and made off in the opposite direction, toward the main road.

"They found Barling lying in his blood, apparently dead; he had been stabbed twice. His injuries were serious, but not fatal. Next day he was able to state that the man who had knifed him was George Jackson, who had done time for forgery. We looked him up in the Rogue's Gallery, and showed the two witnesses his picture, which they recognized at once. Barling refuses to say anything more."

Trent, his elbows on the table, had followed this terse narrative with kindling eyes. "And Jackson is still on the run?"

"He is. He probably slowed down when he got to the main road, seeing he wasn't being pursued; and he could have boarded any one of a dozen buses or trams. It was easy for him to vanish. His description has gone out, of course, with his prison photo; but there's no trace of him as yet. As we knew his real name and history, Dr. Kozicki was called on and interrogated; but he could tell us nothing—didn't even know his son was at liberty, he says. He had had six months knocked off his sentence, you see, for being a good boy. He shed his virtue with his convict's uniform—they often do—"

Trent eyed the inspector thoughtfully for a few moments, then looked away. "It all fits in," he said as if to himself. "I don't like it, but it can't be helped."

"What's on your mind?" Mr. Bligh demanded. "Is it another of your bright ideas? They are usually worth something, so let's have it."

"Well, I have an idea—I don't know if you'll call it a bright one—about where you can lay hands on your man. But it means more tragedy for someone, if I'm right."

"It'll mean tragedy for you, my lad, if you connive at the escape of a dangerous criminal," the inspector said briskly, drawing his chair up to the table. "Come on; let's hear it."

Trent let him hear it.

At the corner of Reville Place the next morning Trent met Mr. Bligh, who was followed at some distance by another plain-clothes officer, already known to Trent as Sergeant Borrett. A closed car was waiting there, and as they passed it the inspector and its driver exchanged almost imperceptible nods.

"You've told her what to do?" Mr. Bligh asked.

"She will have got my letter this morning," Trent said. "As we arranged, I didn't tell her anything—only asked her to leave at her usual time, not to take any notice of us when she sees us at the door, and to go straight off to her job as if nothing was happening."

"Right."

They came to the door of No. 43, and Trent opened it with Marion's latchkey. When the sergeant had joined them in the entry, they went quickly up to the top floor and waited before the entrance to the flat. "Probably nothing will happen until she's been gone some time," the inspector remarked, "but we don't want to have this door opening and shutting more than it usually does."

At nine-fifteen precisely Marion, equipped with hat and handbag, opened the entrance door and came out. She was flushed and bright-eyed as she took in the sight of the three tall figures waiting on the stair-head. "I got your note," she murmured to Trent; then hurried down below.

The three men entered quietly, shutting the door behind them, however, not so quietly. Mr. Bligh, after a glance into each of the four rooms that opened upon the landing, led the way into the largest, the living room in which Trent had listened to Marion's story; and there they waited in silence with the room door open, for what seemed to Trent the longest half-hour his watch had ever told.

At last a sharp, slight noise came from without, and the inspector motioned the others to stand farther back from the door. Other faint sounds followed; and then there came into view through the doorway an object which was slowly descending from the ceiling outside the room. It was a small suitcase, dangling from a cord fastened to its handle. This came noiselessly to rest on the landing; the cord dropped beside it; and then with a dry rattle, a rope ladder with rungs of cane unrolled itself swiftly from above until its end just cleared the floor.

The ladder began to thrash about and to creak, and two feet appeared. A man was feeling his way down by this awkward means; a short, strongly-made man with disproportionately broad shoulders. But just before the head on the shoulders came into the watchers' field of vision the two officers were out of the room with a rush.

The man was instantly dragged from the ladder. There followed a furious and wordless struggle, during which a small hall table and the bowl of flowers upon it were smashed to pieces, and a panel of the entrance door was cracked by a boot heel. At last the handcuffs snapped, and George Jackson was formally acquainted with the reason for his arrest as he stood glowering and panting in the secure grasp of Sergeant Borrett.

Jackson's broad, high forehead and overdeveloped jaws made his face almost square; his lips were thin, his chin was short, his narrow-lidded eyes were much too far apart, and he was villainously unshaven.

Mr. Bligh jerked an automatic pistol from the captive's breastpocket.

"You see," he remarked to Trent, "there couldn't have been a better way of getting him. If he'd had his hands free, somebody might have been hurt with his Betsy before he could be stopped. If we had tried to get him in that loft, somebody would have been killed pretty certainly, and he could have stood the whole Force off up there, so long as he had food and ammunition. But if he was making use of the flat, there had to be a rope or a ladder of some kind; and while he was coming down he was helpless."

He went to the window opening onto the street, put his head out and waved a hand. The car at the corner rolled gently up to No. 43.

"Take him along, Borrett," Mr. Bligh said, opening the entrance door. "I'll be over when I have had a look round up above."

The sergeant twined one fist scientifically into Jackson's collar, the other into a sleeve, and propelled him at arm's length through the doorway and down the stairs. From first to last he had not spoken a word.

"First we'll have a look at his traveling outfit," Mr. Bligh said, as he slipped the catches of the suitcase on the floor. "Good idea, that—saved a lot of climbing up and down. What have we here? Toothbrush, soap, and towel, brush and comb —he has nice, clean habits, anyhow, and didn't like to use anything of Miss Silvester's more than he had to. He was able to wash regularly and leave no traces—have a bath, too. No shaving tackle—as you might expect from the look of him."

"That was the notion, I think," Trent said. "To lie low—or rather high—until the hunt for him had cooled off, and meanwhile grow a beard and mustache that would be a better disguise than anything else. What's that you've got there?"

The inspector held it up, eyeing it appreciatively. "Boned chicken in glass—none of your vulgar tins. Tomato soup in bottle. Biscuits, butter—his old man was doing him well, I must say. Salt and pepper, packet of tea. Two cloths—for washing up, I suppose, so as not to use Miss Silvester's. He must have made free with her plates and knives and forks and kitchen things, though; there's none of them here. By the way, she may notice a rise in her gas bill, if Jackson has been using the cooker as well as the kitchen and bathroom geysers, and the gas fire in the sitting room. I should say he was very comfortable here, making himself quite at home for eight hours or so a day."

"And at intervals the doctor would look in with fresh supplies," Trent remarked. "That would be when he was supposed to be attending patients at their own homes, no doubt."

The inspector closed the suitcase and rose from his knees. "I'm glad his old man supplied a ladder. It will be easier than a rope for anybody my size."

"It will certainly be easier than the way Jackson first got up into the loft," Trent remarked, "if I am right in thinking they dragged the living room table on to the landing and put a chair on top of it. Jackson would only just be able to push up the trapdoor with his fingers, and hauling himself up required some strength. The scratches made by the feet of the chair gave me an idea almost at the start."

"But that wasn't all you had to go on?" suggested the inspector.

"No. Before that, I thought the doctor must have some reason for manufacturing a job for a girl he didn't know, and keeping her safe in his own house all day. What he did know was that she lived in a top-floor flatlet; and he visited her once to see if the usual loft and trapdoor were where they could be made use of. When she started work with him, he borrowed the keys from her bag at the first opportunity, took a squeeze of them, and filed duplicates from a couple of Yale blanks— he's quite a craftsman, I'm told. Then he laid in the necessary stores, and one evening when Miss Silvester was at the theater with his daughter he met Ladislas, brought him here, and left him settled in under the roof. That's my story, anyhow. I've thought over it a lot since yesterday, and that's how I fill in the outlines."

Mr. Bligh grunted. "It must have been something like that. Of course he knew his son was released as soon as it happened. Probably he got the doctor on the phone and arranged a meeting somewhere. He may have told him what he meant to do to Whimster. He must have told him he was going to be wanted by the police again, and must have a safe hideout. Then the doctor was struck by a notion, and he began working on the plan for making a hideout of the loft over his daughter's friend's place. A good plan, too."

"Perhaps he didn't need to be told what a lad like that was going to do to the man who put him away," Trent suggested. "If you're a Pole, as well as a wrong 'un, you are not apt to have a forgiving nature. If it was a question of saving his son from a hanging, I suppose he was ready for anything."

"Well, he'll get plenty, I daresay—though there'll be sympathy for him, too. Now will you hold on to the foot of this ladder while I go up? If you want to come, you'll have to manage by yourself, as Jackson did."

"If I want to come?"

By the light of the inspector's big electric torch they surveyed the sleeping quarters of the *soi-disant* George Jackson. Between two of the roof beams a light canvas hammock was slung, folded blankets within it. Some sheets of pasteboard had been laid over the ceiling joists in one corner, and on them stood an array of preserved foods, a tin of biscuits, a carton of eggs, a packet of candles, and other household necessaries. In another corner was a pile of newspapers.

"Nothing to sit on," Trent observed. "You can't carry a chair about the streets without exciting remark—besides, there's nowhere for a chair to stand. No wonder he had a fondness for that armchair below."

"It must have taken the doctor several visits to get this place furnished," the inspector said. "Well, I've seen enough. I'll have all this removed before Miss Silvester comes home. I wonder how she'll like it when you tell her the story. It'll be something for her to talk about for the rest of her life—how she had a young man staying in her flat for a fortnight without knowing it."

When they had made the descent, Trent turned to gathering up the wreckage on the floor and stowing it in a corner of the kitchen.

"I shall have to get Marion a new table and bowl," he remarked. "I promised her I wouldn't smash up the furniture." He laughed suddenly.

Mr. Bligh inquired what the joke was.

"Why, I just remembered," Trent said, "that she told me this wasn't one of my crime problems."

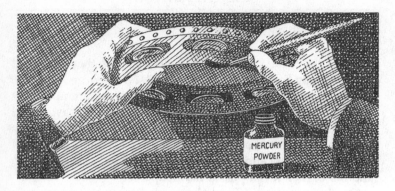

FINGERPRINTING A GHOST

TONY FLETCHER

from Memories of Murder

I thought it would be interesting to have a true story in this collection, and this one comes from the memories of a fingerprint expert. We've all seen, in a hundred different films and TV series, the scene-of-crime officers dusting the door handle (or the handle of a dagger) with special powder and lifting off the prints of the murderer. Tony Fletcher was a police fingerprint specialist for many years, and in this story he tells of the difficulties the police faced when they tried to fingerprint a disembodied spirit. In the absence of a body, how could there be any fingerprints?

But there certainly seemed to be a hand . . .

FEW OF US, when looking back at our working life, will have no regrets; something we did which perhaps we should not have done or a chance we had and turned down. I still regret that during my police service I refused to tackle a job of work which was unique, would have proved most interesting, and required but little time and effort. The request was for me to fingerprint a ghost. I refused because I did not believe in ghosts and I considered at the time that the attempt would make me appear foolish. How I wish that opportunity would present itself again.

In the spring of 1961 I was working in the bureau alongside a close friend whom I had known since my C Division days. There was a knock on the door and in came David Cohen, a middle-aged gentleman. He told us he was secretary of the Manchester branch of the Psychical Research Society.

Although this society has always taken itself and its work seriously, many people at the time did not. I believe that their purpose has always been to investigate phenomena which have no obvious explanation, to eliminate the possibility of trickery and to do this in as scientific a manner as possible, keeping careful records and statements of witnesses. The last twenty years or so have seen tremendous changes in the attitudes toward this kind of work by scientists and members of the public. Indeed, the late Arthur Koestler, scientist, philosopher, writer, indeed polymath, left sufficient money in his will for the funding of a Chair in Psychical Research at one of our universities.

Mr. Cohen asked for the services of an expert to fingerprint a pair of hands which were appearing during seances held in a small house in South Manchester, and to assist in inquiries he was making as the result of certain manifestations. He went on to explain that in his official position as secretary of the society he had been approached some two years previously by a woman who had an intriguing story to tell. She lived in a small terraced house on the southern side of the city. She had a teenage son, a younger daughter, and had recently been widowed. She spoke of mysterious happenings in her home for which she could not find any logical explanation.

Her son was taking violin lessons, and shortly after the death of her husband she woke one night to the sound of a violin being played. She got out of bed and went to her son's bedroom, expecting to see him playing. The music stopped just before she reached his room. She opened the door only to find him peacefully asleep in his bed and nothing untoward to be seen.

She returned to her room somewhat troubled and tried to

convince herself she had been dreaming. Over a period of time the incident was frequently repeated. Always there was the sound of a violin being played in her son's bedroom, and she always found her son fast asleep. The music was always the same, Ravel's Bolero.

Several months later, fearing she was on the edge of a nervous breakdown and believing the music to be part of her imagination, after yet another disturbed night, she asked her son if he had been awake during the night playing his violin, even though she knew the intricacies of such a piece were well beyond his ability. His answer astounded her: "Oh, no, it was not me playing the violin, it was Nicholas."

When she had recovered her composure she asked her son who Nicholas was. He said, "Nicholas is the old man who plays the violin for me." Somewhat reassured as to her sanity, despite great uncertainties about what had actually happened, she went to see Mr. Cohen and asked if his society could help to lay the ghost, if that was what it was.

Mr. Cohen set to work. He and other selected members held a number of seances at the small house in Fallowfield. The point had now been reached where contact with Nicholas had been established and during one part of the seance, held in a darkened room, a pair of hands had manifested themselves. This had become a regular occurrence and the reason Mr. Cohen was seeking our services was quite simple, and quite in accordance with the society's wish to eliminate all trickery: he wished the expert to come along and attend a seance. If the opportunity presented itself he was to fingerprint the hands. If he was successful, the next step would be to fingerprint every person present in the room. By comparing all these it was hoped to eliminate any suspicion and confirm that there was indeed another presence in the room.

Mr. Cohen could see I was a doubting Thomas and was not in the least surprised when I refused my services. However, he appeared so genuine that I felt the least I could do would be to take his name and address and pass on his request to another member of the bureau, Sergeant Rowland Mason, a close friend and fingerprint expert of great ability.

A few words about Rowly Mason would not go amiss. He was an exceptional man in many ways, not least in the fingerprint business. He often seemed to have had a sixth sense about a culprit even when we had so little to go on that we had almost given up. Perhaps his past experiences had to some extent honed his senses. Born in 1919, the son of a Manchester policeman, he had flown thirty-four missions as a rear gunner with the Royal Air Force during the war. That alone makes him special, because very few flew so many with Bomber Command. The chances of surviving as Tail End Charlie in a Lancaster on a bombing raid were not good at their best; to survive ten trips was really going it; to survive the number Rowland did was bordering on the miraculous. The experience left him patient, philosophical, generally very cheerful, and with a liking for life, a turn of wit, and a wry attitude toward minor peccadilloes, but a burning dislike of real evil. We all liked him and he had many friends throughout the force. Better on your side than on the other fellow's!

Rowland eventually consented to meet Mr. Cohen and attempt to fingerprint the ghost. I remember the look on his face when he said, "The difficult we do today; the impossible we'll try tomorrow."

He met Mr. Cohen and it was agreed he would attend a number of seances. He was to use the first two to assess the situation and any difficulties which lay ahead. In the office after each seance he gave a full report to the attentive audience, before work in the bureau was allowed to commence. Not surprisingly, there was a certain amount of chaffing, but at the same time there was keen interest in deciding what the technical approach should be.

If my memory serves me well, the people attending the seances were the widow of the household, her son, and Mr. Cohen; the only variation being whoever came from the society to act as observer and Sergeant Mason, the practiced taker of genuine, earthly fingerprints.

At the first meeting Sergeant Mason was introduced to the other members of the party and it was explained to them that he had a plan of campaign. With the room in darkness and everybody sitting around a table, the "spirit," Nicholas, confirmed his presence by a series of knocks. There was a fine example of levitation when the large table around which the people were sitting rose in the air to such a height that Rowland had to stand on tiptoe, with arm outstretched, before he could touch the top of it; and Rowland is a tall chap.

Later, a tambourine which had previously been painted with luminous paint, flew about the room at incredible speeds, constantly changing direction as it did so and in a way which no human earthly agency could have achieved.

Next morning at the bureau Rowland informed us all that he was completely mystified by the previous evening's events, and could not offer any logical explanation. Knowing him as we all did, respecting his professional abilities and his undoubted skill at sniffing out the less than obvious clue, we had to believe him.

A second visit to the Fallowfield house provided more mystery and suspense. Not only was there loud knocking on the table, accompanied by violent shaking and a degree of levitation, but after the tambourine had flown around the darkened sitting room a pair of hands manifested themselves. As the room was in total darkness it would not be right to say that the hands appeared, but Sergeant Mason said they were certainly there. Mr. Cohen had described them as dry and scaly, and as having lace cuffs over the wrists.

What Rowland felt was touches on his shoulder and arms. He was absolutely sure that he was not being touched by any person present. Later he touched the hands himself.

During the course of a long career Sergeant Mason has, like every other fingerprint expert, held hands in the nicest possible way with the quick and the dead, the guilty and the innocent, the young, the middle-aged, and the elderly, the willing and the unwilling. He simply says that the hands were a little dry and fairly slim. When telling us this the following morning there was, of course, some good-humored banter, but there was not one member of the department who was not intrigued by the happenings, and nobody for one moment thought that Sergeant Mason was imagining things.

He decided that on his third visit he would try to take the fingerprints of the ghost or the human being responsible for creating the illusion, and to accomplish this he was prepared to enter into a little legitimate deception. He would not do the obvious, which would be to grasp the hands and attempt to fingerprint them, but would use the scenes-of-crime technique. He got to the house on the Friday evening well ahead of the others in order to prepare the scene. He was equipped with brushes, mercury powder (which is the best type of fingerprint powder, only to be used with extreme care on special occasions), and a duster. He went into the living room and, without telling anybody, removed the tambourine from its place on the sideboard. Using his duster, he carefully polished it to make sure that it was clean, shining, and free of fingerprints, providing what he hoped would be an ideal surface. Then he put his duster by the side of the sideboard.

As soon as the other people had gathered, the seance began. The householder, acting as the medium, took charge of the proceedings. The room was darkened and all present were seated around the table. Suddenly Rowland was struck by a soft object. His hair stood on end on the back of his neck. He was rather shocked to find that the duster he had used to clean the tambourine had been flung in his face, but by whom? No human person knew what he had done, but something was letting him know he had been observed.

The events which followed were much as before—violent knockings, levitation, being touched by hands, and the tambourine flying wildly around the room; one difference was that the householder played a tape of Ravel's Bolero. After the meeting had ended and the lights were switched on every person appeared to be seated in his or her normal position. Rowland took immediate possession of the tambourine and carefully dusted it with fingerprint powder, hoping to develop and recover a set of prints. The tambourine was as clean and free from fingerprints as when he had polished it an hour previously!

On a further visit the tambourine was powdered with the fingerprint material before the seance began. The tambourine was seen to rise from the sideboard and circle the room; all observed this. Afterwards the powder which had been brushed on to it was found apparently undisturbed. The mystery deepened.

As the hands were now manifesting themselves on a regular basis it was decided to ascertain whether the spirit Nicholas would be agreeable to having his fingerprints taken. Through a series of questions answered by knocks, the answer was yes. Rowland decided to try using the clean print method. Whereas one normally rolls the fingers on a plate covered by a thin layer of printer's ink and then transfers the prints onto paper, the clean print method entails placing the fingers onto a chemically charged pad and, after removing them, touching them on sensitized paper. This ensures a reasonably good print without dirtying the hand. It was decided to do this the following week, and was to prove most difficult.

Rowland had to put the chemically charged pad and the sensitized paper on the table directly in front of him. In complete darkness he had to make contact with one of the ghostly hands; then he had to hold this hand in one of his own, and with the other find the fingerprint pad, guide the spirit's hand to the pad, and make sure that the tips of the fingers touched it, feel for the sensitized paper, and complete the operation by putting the spirit's chemically treated fingers onto the paper—under the circumstances, not an easy task.

However, all went fairly well. In the course of the seance, with the agreement of Nicholas, Rowland caught hold of one of the hands; in the pitch darkness he could feel that it was dry. With his other hand he guided the hand to the fingerprint pad and touched it. Now he had to seek the sensitized paper and bring the apparition's hand into contact with it. This he believed he had achieved.

Next morning he arrived at the bureau with the sensitized paper. The whole staff were agog. The paper was carefully examined. It revealed three one-inch-long scratch marks, each parallel with the others. They could have been made by a bird's claw; they could equally have been made by three fingernails scratching the paper. There were no identifiable fingerprints.

More seances were held and the incidents re-enacted the following morning in the bureau (to the accompaniment of Ravel's Bolero) for the benefit of a most receptive and expert audience. It was agreed that the police photographer should be approached to see if he could photograph the ghost or indeed any events connected with it. Constable John Cheetham, a photographer of great experience, confirmed the possibility of taking photographs using infrared light, and what was more he would be prepared to try this if he could first attend a seance and check that the circumstances and events outlined by Rowland were indeed true.

On Rowland's next visit to the Fallowfield house he was accompanied not only by John Cheetham but also by John's wife, Flo. Next morning at the office John confirmed that there certainly were mysterious happenings at the house. There had been loud knockings, levitation, and the tambourine had flown around the room; further, he and his wife had each been touched by what felt like two hands. Not only did he confirm everything Rowland had said, all of it defying logical explanation, but said that his wife was so frightened that she would never under any circumstances be prepared to enter the room again.

Before describing further events I must mention that while John Cheetham and his wife had been present a vase of flowers was standing well away from the table around which they were sitting; the flowers themselves were taken out of the vase and scattered around the room. Another point, and I gather the same condition has applied to hundreds of other such cases, is that the temperature often varied; these were fairly warm summer evenings and yet the temperature would drop to freezing. The music, too, was strange. It had been recorded on tape in a perfectly orthodox manner, but when it was played at these seances it would vary from very soft to deafeningly loud.

Rowland had always been a sort of elder brother figure in the bureau, and of course no one could match either his Air Force or his working experience, or his instinct for the job. Nobody was bantering now after all these weeks of patient and serious investigation.

At the seance attended by John Cheetham and his wife, by the usual system of questions answered by knocks, Nicholas the ghost was asked whether he would be prepared to sit in an armchair and be photographed. Yes, he would.

Events the following Friday went exactly as planned. The camera was set, focused on the armchair which had been placed in position. The room was darkened, the medium contacted the spirit and requested it to occupy the chair. The photograph was taken.

Next morning found everybody eagerly awaiting the development of the negative. When the photographs arrived they showed a chair, resting against the back of which was a large creased cushion. Nothing else.

However, the older reader will recall the pastime of staring into a glowing coal fire and seeing an image, probably an image of what you wanted to see. Now, as each police officer present stared at that creased cushion he could see the image of the face of a very old man, bearded and turned to the right, rather like the head of the old king on a coin. I could see it and I could describe it. So could the others. It was a remarkable coincidence that all present could see the same thing.

The experiment soon came to an abrupt end. Somehow, and I suppose it was inevitable, the story leaked out to the press. A full account of the events and the police involvement in them was printed in the *Daily Mail*. Although no police time was involved in the investigation, the Chief Superintendent in charge of the CID demanded that the two officers concerned should submit lengthy and comprehensive reports. They both did so, not withholding any of the details. Nothing further was heard and the events are but a memory.

If you were now to ask me if I believe in ghosts, I would reply that I do not readily disbelieve in the supernatural and that there are probably two reports still on file in police archives which bear witness to the events I have just related. Nobody was pulling anyone's leg about any of it, except perhaps Nicholas—and even he seemed to be perfectly serious. I am told that manifestations such as this often occur when there is a juvenile living in the house. Sometimes such juveniles have been found to be responsible for trickery. False or real, the phenomenon is known and recognized all over the world, particularly in Europe, and has been so for hundreds of years. I am sure that the teenage boy in this house in Fallowfield had nothing to do with the events which Rowland Mason described to us, that all concerned were perfectly serious in intent, and that no trickery was used. Mr. Cohen also seemed satisfied in this respect, but of course could not give any explanation beyond, perhaps, the wish of the long-dead Nicholas to have a part in present life through the agency, somehow, of the boy. No more can be said by me, except that I fervently wish I had not turned down the opportunity when it was presented. There is so much we do not know, perhaps never will know, and maybe never should know. There is an old saying that there is nothing new under the sun; true, I suppose. What is new is that scientists are now asking different questions and have much improved technology to help find the answers. It may be that the new Chair at Edinburgh, funded by the late Arthur Koestler, will provide some answers to such questions.

IT'S A HARD WORLD

ANDREW VACHSS

Modern crime fiction depicts a doubt-filled, shadowy world where the good guys and the bad guys are hard to tell from one another. This is a story told from the point of view of a man on the run. We don't know what he's done, but we know we don't want the two flat-faced men in the corner to nail him. But in the brightly lit bustle of a busy airport, where can he hide?

Luckily, a solution slams right into him—if he can use it.

I PULLED INTO the parking lot at LaGuardia around noon and sat in the car running my fingers over the newly tightened skin on my face, trying to think through my next move. I couldn't count on the plastic surgery to do the job. I had to get out of New York at least long enough to see if DellaCroce's people still were looking for me.

I sat there for an hour or so thinking it through, but nothing came to me. Time to move. I left the car where it was—let Hertz pick it up in a week or so when I didn't turn it in.

The Delta terminal was all by itself in a corner of the airport. I had a ticket for Augusta, Georgia, by way of Atlanta. Canada was where I had to go if I wanted to get out of the country, but Atlanta gave me a lot of options. The airport there is the size of a small city; it picks up traffic from all over the country.

I waited until the last minute to board, but it was quiet and peaceful. They didn't have anybody on the plane with me. Plenty of time to think; maybe too much time. A running man sticks out too much. I had to find a way out of this soon or DellaCroce would nail me when I ran out of places to hide.

Atlanta Airport was the usual mess: travelers running through the tunnels, locals selling everything from shoe shines to salvation. I had a couple of hours until the connecting flight to Augusta, so I found a pay phone and called the Blind Man in New York.

"What's the story?" I asked, not identifying myself.

"Good news and bad news, pal," came back the Blind Man's harsh whisper. He'd spent so much time in solitary back when we did time together that his eyes were bad and his voice had rusted from lack of practice. "They got the name that's on your ticket, but no pictures."

"Damn! How did they get on the ticket so fast?"

"What's the difference, pal? Dump the ticket and get the hell out of there."

"And do what?"

"You got me, brother. But be quick or be dead," said the Blind Man, breaking the connection.

The first thing I did was get out of the Delta area. I went to the United counter and booked a flight to Chicago, leaving in three hours. You have to stay away from borders when you're paying cash for an airline ticket, but I didn't see any obvious DEA agents lurking around and, anyway, I wasn't carrying luggage.

With the Chicago ticket tucked safely away in my pocket, I drifted slowly back toward the boarding area for the Augusta flight. It was getting near to departure time. I found myself a seat in the waiting area, lit a cigarette, and kept an eye on the people at the ticketing desk. There was a short walkway to the plane, with a pretty little blonde standing there checking off the boarding passes. Still peaceful, the silence routinely interrupted by the usual airport announcements, but no tension. It felt right to me. Maybe I'd try for Augusta after all; I hate Chicago when it's cold.

And then I spotted the hunters: two flat-faced men sitting in a corner of the waiting area. Sitting so close their shoulders were touching, they both had their eyes pinned on the little blonde, not sweeping the room like I would have expected. But I knew who they were. You don't survive a dozen years behind the walls if you can't tell the hunters from the herd.

They wouldn't be carrying; bringing handguns into an airport was too much of a risk. Besides, their job was to point the finger, not pull the trigger. I saw how they planned to work it; they had the walkway boxed in. But I didn't see what good it would do them if they couldn't put a face on their target.

The desk man announced the boarding of Flight 884 to Augusta. I sat there like it was none of my business, not moving. One by one, the passengers filed into the narrow area. The sweet southern voice of the blonde piped up, "Pleased to have you with us today, Mr. Wilson," and my eyes flashed over to the hunters. Sure enough, they were riveted to the blonde's voice. She called off the name of each male passenger as he filed past her. If the women passengers felt slighted at the lack of recognition, they kept quiet about it. A perfect trap: if I put my body through that walkway, the little blonde would brand the name they already had to my new face, and I'd be dead meat as soon as the plane landed.

I got up to get away from there just as the desk man called out, "Last call for Flight 884." They couldn't have watchers at all the boarding areas. I'd just have to get to Chicago, call the Blind Man, and try and work something out. As I walked past the desk, a guy slammed into me. He bounced back a few feet, put a nasty expression on his face, and then dropped it when he saw mine. A clown in his late thirties, trying to pass for a much younger guy: hair carefully styled forward to cover a receding hairline, silk shirt open to mid-chest, fancy sunglasses dangling from a gold chain around his neck. I moved away slowly and watched as he approached the desk.

"I got a ticket for this flight," he barked out, like he was used to being obeyed.

"Of course, sir. May I see your boarding pass?"

"I don't have a goddamn pass. Can't I get one here?"

"I'm sorry, sir," the desk man told him, "the flight is all boarded at this time. We have four more boarding passes outstanding. We can certainly issue one to you, but it has to be on what we call the 'modified standby' basis. If the people holding boarding passes don't show up five minutes before flight time, we will call your name and give you the pass."

"What kind of crap is this?" the clown demanded. "I paid good money for this ticket."

"I'm sure you did, sir. But that's the procedure. I'm sure you won't have any trouble boarding. This happens all the time on these short flights. Just give us your ticket, and we'll call you by name just before the flight leaves, all right?"

I guess it wasn't all right, but the clown had no choice. He slammed his ticket down on the counter, tossed his leather jacket casually over one shoulder, and took a seat near the desk.

It wasn't a great shot, but it was the best one I'd had in a while. I waited a couple of heartbeats and followed the clown to the desk. I listened patiently to their explanation, left my ticket, and was told that they would call me by name when my turn came.

I didn't have much time. I walked over to where the clown was sitting, smoking a cigarette like he'd invented it. "Look," I told him, "I need to get on that flight to Augusta. It's important to me. Business reasons."

"So what's that to me?" he smirked, shrugging his shoulders.

"I know you got ahead of me on the list, okay? It's worth a hundred to me to change places with you. Let me go when your name is called, and you can go when they call mine, if they do," I told him, taking out a pair of fifties and holding them out to him.

His eyes lit up. I could see the wheels turning in his head. He knew a sucker when he saw one. "What if we both get on?" he wanted to know.

"That's my tough luck," I said. "I need to do everything possible to get on the flight. It's important to me."

He appeared to hesitate, but it was no contest. "My name's Morrison," he said, taking the fifties from my hand. "Steele," I said, and walked toward the desk.

The watchers hadn't looked at us. A couple of minutes passed. I gently worked myself away from the clown, watching the watchers. The desk man piped up: "Mr. Morrison, Mr. Albert Morrison, we have your boarding pass." I shot up from my seat, grabbed the pass, and hit the walkway. The little blonde sang out, "Have a pleasant flight, Mr. Morrison," as I passed. I could feel the heat of the hunters' eyes on my back.

I wasn't fifty feet into the runway when I heard, "Mr. Steele, Mr. Henry Steele, we have your boarding pass." I kept going and found my seat in the front of the plane.

I watched the aisle and, sure enough, the clown passed me by, heading for the smoking section in the rear. I thought he winked at me, but I couldn't be sure.

The flight to Augusta was only half an hour, but the plane couldn't outrun a phone call. The airport was a tiny thing, just one building, with a short walk to the cabs outside. The clown passed by me as I was heading outside, bumped me with his shoulder, held up my two fifties in his hand, and gave me a greasy smile. "It's a hard world," he said, moving out ahead of me.

I watched as two men swung in behind him. One was carrying a golf bag; the other had his hands free.

MADDENED BY MYSTERY

STEPHEN LEACOCK

To end with, here is a parody of the classic detective story by the Canadian writer Stephen Leacock. Absurdity can go no further than it does in his Nonsense Novels, *which mock all kinds of literary genres. His satire on the detective story has everything: disguises, disappearances, and a death—though the death comes at the very end, and is entirely comic.*

THE GREAT DETECTIVE sat in his office. He wore a long green gown and half a dozen secret badges pinned to the outside of it.

Three or four pairs of false whiskers hung on a whisker-stand beside him.

Goggles, blue spectacles, and motor glasses lay within easy reach.

He could completely disguise himself at a second's notice.

His face was absolutely impenetrable.

A pile of cryptograms lay on the desk. The Great Detective hastily tore them open one after the other, solved them, and threw them down the cryptogram chute at his side.

There was a rap at the door.

The Great Detective hurriedly wrapped himself in a pink

domino, adjusted a pair of false black whiskers, and cried, "Come in."

His secretary entered. "Ha," said the detective, "it is you!" He laid aside his disguise.

"Sir," said the young man in intense excitement, "a mystery has been committed!"

"Ha!" said the Great Detective, his eye kindling, "is it such as to completely baffle the police of the entire continent?"

"They are so completely baffled with it," said the secretary, "that they are lying collapsed in heaps; many of them have committed suicide."

"So," said the detective, "and is the mystery one that is absolutely unparalleled in the whole recorded annals of the London police?"

"It is."

"And I suppose," said the detective, "that it involves names which you would scarcely dare to breathe, at least without first using some kind of atomizer or throat-gargle."

"Exactly."

"And it is connected, I presume, with the highest diplomatic consequences, so that if we fail to solve it England will be at war with the whole world in sixteen minutes?"

His secretary, still quivering with excitement, again answered yes.

"And finally," said the Great Detective, "I presume that it was committed in broad daylight, in some such place as the entrance of the Bank of England, or in the cloakroom of the House of Commons, and under the very eyes of the police?"

"Those," said the secretary, "are the very conditions of the mystery."

"Good," said the Great Detective, "now wrap yourself in this disguise, put on these brown whiskers, and tell me what it is."

The secretary wrapped himself in a blue domino with lace insertions, then, bending over, he whispered in the ear of the Great Detective:

"The Prince of Wurttemberg has been kidnapped."

The Great Detective bounded from his chair as if he had

been kicked from below.

A prince stolen! Evidently a Bourbon! The scion of one of the oldest families in Europe kidnapped. Here was a mystery indeed worthy of his analytical brain.

His mind began to move like lightning.

"Stop!" he said, "how do you know this?"

The secretary handed him a telegram. It was from the Prefect of Police of Paris. It read: "The Prince of Wurttemberg stolen. Probably forwarded to London. Must have him here for the opening day of Exhibition. £1,000 reward."

So! The Prince had been kidnapped out of Paris at the very time when his appearance at the International Exposition would have been a political event of the first magnitude.

With the Great Detective to think was to act, and to act was to think. Frequently he could do both together.

"Wire to Paris for a description of the Prince."

The secretary bowed and left.

At the same moment there was a slight scratching at the door.

A visitor entered. He crawled stealthily on his hands and knees. A hearthrug thrown over his head and shoulders disguised his identity.

He crawled to the middle of the room.

Then he rose.

Great Heaven!

It was the Prime Minister of England.

"You!" said the detective.

"Me," said the Prime Minister.

"You have come in regard to the kidnapping of the Prince of Wurttemberg?"

The Prime Minister started.

"How do you know?" he said.

The Great Detective smiled his inscrutable smile.

"Yes," said the Prime Minister. "I will use no concealment. I am interested, deeply interested. Find the Prince of Wurttemberg, get him safe back to Paris, and I will add £500 to the reward already offered. But listen," he said impressively as he left the room, "see to it that no attempt is made to alter the marking of the Prince, or to clip his tail."

So! To clip the Prince's tail! The brain of the Great Detective reeled. So! a gang of miscreants had conspired to—but no! the thing was not possible.

There was another rap at the door.

A second visitor was seen. He wormed his way in, lying almost prone upon his stomach, and wriggling across the floor. He was enveloped in a long purple cloak. He stood up and peeped over the top of it.

Great Heaven!

It was the Archbishop of Canterbury!

"Your Grace!" exclaimed the detective in amazement—"pray do not stand, I beg you. Sit down, lie down, anything rather than stand."

The Archbishop took off his mitre and laid it wearily on the whisker-stand.

"You are here in regard to the Prince of Wurttemberg."

The Archbishop started and crossed himself. Was the man a magician?

"Yes," he said, "much depends on getting him back. But I have only come to say this: my sister is desirous of seeing you. She is coming here. She has been extremely indiscreet and her fortune hangs upon the Prince. Get him back to Paris or I fear she will be ruined."

The Archbishop regained his mitre, uncrossed himself, wrapped his cloak about him, and crawled stealthily out on his hands and knees, purring like a cat.

The face of the Great Detective showed the most profound sympathy. It ran up and down in furrows. "So," he muttered, "the sister of the Archbishop, the Countess of Dashleigh!" Accustomed as he was to the life of the aristocracy, even the Great Detective felt that there was here intrigue of more than customary complexity.

There was a loud rapping at the door.

There entered the Countess of Dashleigh. She was all in furs. She was the most beautiful woman in England. She strode imperiously into the room. She seized a chair imperiously and seated herself on it, imperial side up.

She took off her tiara of diamonds and put it on the tiara-holder beside her and uncoiled her boa of pearls and put it on the pearl-stand.

"You have come," said the Great Detective, "about the Prince of Wurttemberg."

"Wretched little pup!" said the Countess of Dashleigh in disgust.

So! A further complication! Far from being in love with the Prince, the Countess denounced the young Bourbon as a pup!

"You are interested in him, I believe."

"Interested!" said the Countess. "I should rather say so. Why, I bred him!"

"You which?" gasped the Great Detective, his usually impassive features suffused with a carmine blush.

"I bred him," said the Countess, "and I've got £10,000 upon his chances, so no wonder I want him back in Paris. Only listen," she said, "if they've got hold of the Prince and cut his tail or spoiled the markings of his stomach it would be far better to have him quietly put out of the way here."

The Great Detective reeled and leaned up against the side of the room. So! The cold-blooded admission of the beautiful woman for the moment took away his breath! Herself the mother of the young Bourbon, misallied with one of the greatest families of Europe, staking her fortune on a Royalist plot, and yet with so instinctive a knowledge of European politics as to know that any removal of the hereditary birthmarks of the Prince would forfeit for him the sympathy of the French populace.

The Countess resumed her tiara.

She left.

The secretary re-entered.

"I have three telegrams from Paris," he said, "they are completely baffling."

He handed over the first telegram.

It read:

"The Prince of Wurttemberg has a long, wet snout, broad ears, very long body, and short hind legs."

The Great Detective looked puzzled.

He read the second telegram.

"The Prince of Wurttemberg is easily recognized by his deep bark."

And then the third.

"The Prince of Wurttemberg can be recognized by the patch of white hair across the center of his back."

The two men looked at one another. The mystery was maddening, impenetrable.

The Great Detective spoke.

"Give me my domino," he said. "These clues must be followed up," then pausing, while his quick brain analyzed and summed up the evidence before him—"a young man," he muttered, "evidently young since described as a 'pup', with a long, wet snout (ha! addicted obviously to drinking), a streak of white hair across his back (a first sign of the results of his abandoned life)—yes, yes," he continued, "with this clue I shall find him easily."

The Great Detective rose.

He wrapped himself in a long black cloak with white whiskers and blue spectacles attached.

Completely disguised, he issued forth.

He began the search.

For four days he visited every corner of London.

He entered every saloon in the city. In each of them he drank a glass of rum. In some of them he assumed the disguise of a sailor. In others he entered as a soldier. Into others he penetrated as a clergyman. His disguise was perfect. Nobody paid any attention to him as long as he had the price of a drink.

The search proved fruitless.

Two young men were arrested under suspicion of being the Prince, only to be released.

The identification was incomplete in each case.

One had a long wet snout but no hair on his back.

The other had hair on his back but couldn't bark.

Neither of them was the young Bourbon.

The Great Detective continued his search.

He stopped at nothing.

Secretly, after nightfall, he visited the home of the Prime Minister. He examined it from top to bottom. He measured all the doors and windows. He took up the flooring. He inspected the plumbing. He examined the furniture. He found nothing.

With equal secrecy he penetrated into the palace of the Archbishop. He examined it from top to bottom. Disguised as a choirboy he took part in the offices of the church. He found nothing.

Still undismayed, the Great Detective made his way into the home of the Countess of Dashleigh. Disguised as a housemaid, he entered the service of the Countess.

Then at last the clue came which gave him a solution to the mystery.

On the wall of the Countess's boudoir was a large framed engraving.

It was a portrait.

Under it was a printed legend:

THE PRINCE OF WURTTEMBERG

The portrait was that of a Dachshund.

The long body, the broad ears, the unclipped tail, the short hind legs—all was there.

In the fraction of a second the lightning mind of the Great Detective had penetrated the whole mystery.

THE PRINCE WAS A DOG!!!!

Hastily throwing a domino over his housemaid's dress, he rushed to the street. He summoned a passing hansom, and in a few moments was at his house.

"I have it," he gasped to his secretary, "the mystery is solved. I have pieced it together. By sheer analysis I have reasoned it out. Listen—hind legs, hair on back, wet snout, pup—eh, what? Does that suggest nothing to you?"

"Nothing," said the secretary; "it seems perfectly hopeless."

The Great Detective, now recovered from his excitement, smiled faintly.

"It means simply this, my dear fellow. The Prince of Wurttemberg is a dog, a prize Dachshund. The Countess of Dashleigh bred him, and he is worth some £25,000 in addition to the prize of £10,000 offered at the Paris dog show. Can you wonder that—"

At that moment the Great Detective was interrupted by the scream of a woman.

"Great Heaven!"

The Countess of Dashleigh dashed into the room.

Her face was wild.

Her tiara was in disorder.

Her pearls were dripping all over the place.

She wrung her hands and moaned.

"They have cut his tail," she gasped, "and taken all the hair off his back. What can I do? I am undone!!"

"Madame," said the Great Detective, calm as a bronze, "do yourself up. I can save you yet."

"You!"

"Me!"

"How?"

"Listen. This is how. The Prince was to have been shown at Paris."

The Countess nodded.

"Your fortune was staked on him?"

The Countess nodded again.

"The dog was stolen, carried to London, his tail cut, and his marks disfigured."

Amazed at the quiet penetration of the Great Detective, the Countess kept on nodding and nodding.

"And you are ruined?"

"I am," she gasped, and sank down on the floor in a heap of pearls.

"Madame," said the Great Detective, "all is not lost."

He straightened himself up to his full height. A look of inflinchable unflexibility flickered over his features.

The honor of England, the fortune of the most beautiful woman in England was at stake.

"I will do it," he murmured.

"Rise, dear lady," he continued. "Fear nothing. I will impersonate the dog!!!"

That night the Great Detective might have been seen on the deck of the Calais packet boat with his secretary. He was on his hands and knees in a long black cloak, and his secretary had him on a short chain.

He barked at the waves exultingly and licked the secretary's hand.

"What a beautiful dog," said the passengers.

The disguise was absolutely complete.

The Great Detective had been coated over with mucilage to which dog hairs had been applied. The markings on his back were perfect. His tail, adjusted with an automatic coupler, moved up and down responsive to every thought. His deep eyes were full of intelligence.

Next day he was exhibited in the Dachshund class at the International show.

He won all hearts.

"*Quel beau chien!*" cried the French people.

"*Ach! was ein Dog!*" cried the Spanish.

The Great Detective took the first prize!

The fortune of the Countess was saved.

Unfortunately as the Great Detective had neglected to pay the dog tax, he was caught and destroyed by the dogcatchers. But that is, of course, quite outside of the present narrative, and is only mentioned as an odd fact in conclusion.

INSPECTOR CRAIG'S
SOLUTIONS

Page 94

1

I shall first show that at least one of A, C is guilty. If B is innocent, then it's obvious that A and/or C is guilty—since by (1), no one other than A, B, C is guilty. If B is guilty, then he must have had an accomplice (since he can't drive), so again A or C must be guilty. So A or C (or both) are guilty. If C is innocent, then A must be a guilty one. On the other hand, if C is guilty, then by statement (2), A is also guilty. Therefore A is guilty.

2

This is even simpler. If A is innocent, then, since C is innocent, B must be guilty—by (1). If A is guilty, then, by (2), he had an accomplice, who couldn't be C—by (3), hence must be B. So in either case, B is guilty.

3

Suppose B were innocent. Then one of the twins must be guilty. This twin must have had an accomplice who couldn't be B hence must have been the other twin. But this is impossible since one of the twins was in Dover at the time. Therefore B is guilty. And since B always works alone, both twins are innocent.

Page 166

1

The prosecutor said, in effect, that the defendant didn't commit the crime alone. The defense attorney denied this, which is tantamount to saying that the defendant *did* commit the crime alone.

2

This is extremely simple. By (1), if A is innocent, then C is guilty (because if A is innocent then the statement, "either A is innocent or B is guilty" is true). By (2), if A is innocent then C is innocent. Therefore if A is innocent, then C is both guilty and innocent, which is impossible. Therefore A must be guilty.

3

The two are B and C; at least one of them must be guilty. For, suppose A is innocent. Then B or C must be guilty by (1). On the other hand suppose A is guilty. If B is guilty, then certainly at least one of B, C is guilty. But suppose that B is innocent. Then A is guilty and B is innocent, hence by (2), C must be guilty, so again either B or C is guilty.

4

We first show that if A is guilty, so is C. Well, suppose A is guilty. Then by (2), either B or C is guilty. If B is innocent, then it must be C who is guilty. But suppose B is guilty. Then A and B are both guilty, hence by (1) C is guilty too. This proves that if A is guilty, so is C. Also, by (3), if C is guilty so is D. Combining these two facts, we see that if A is guilty, so is D. But by (4), if A is innocent, so is D. Therefore, regardless of whether A is guilty or innocent, D must be guilty. So D is definitely guilty. The rest are all doubtful.

ACKNOWLEDGMENTS

The publisher would like to thank the copyright holders for permission to reproduce the following copyright material:

Isaac Asimov· "The Cross of Lorraine," copyright © 1976 by Isaac Asimov, from *Casebook of the Black Widowers* by Isaac Asimov, used by permission of Doubleday, a division of Bantam Doubleday Dell Publishing Group, Inc. **E. C. Bentley:** "The Little Mystery" from *Trent Intervenes* by E. C. Bentley, copyright © 1938 by E. C. Bentley, renewed 1966 by Nicolas Bentley, reprinted by permission of Bella Jones. **Italo Calvino:** "The One-Handed Murderer" from *Italian Folktales: Selected and Retold by Italo Calvino*, copyright © 1956 by Giulio Einaudi editore, s.p.a., English translation by George Martin copyright © 1980 by Harcourt Brace & Company, reprinted by permission of Harcourt Brace & Company. **Leslie Charteris:** "The Newdick Helicopter" from *Boodle* by Leslie Charteris (Hodder & Stoughton Ltd., 1934), copyright © 1934 by Leslie Charteris. **Agatha Christie:** "The Adventures of the Egyptian Tomb" from *Poirot Investigates* by Agatha Christie (1924), reprinted by permission of Hughes Massie Ltd. **Tony Fletcher·** "Fingerprinting a Ghost," an extract from *Memories of Murder—The Great Cases of a Finger-print Expert* by Tony Fletcher (Weidenfeld & Nicolson, 1986) reprinted by permission of the Orion Publishing Group Ltd. **Erich Kästner:** Chapters 3, 5, 6 from *Emil* (including *Emil and the Detectives, Emil and the Three Twins, The Thirty-Fifth of May*) by Erich Kästner, reprinted by permission of Atrium Verlag AG. **Ellery Queen:** "Cold Money" by Ellery Queen, copyright © 1952 by Ellery Queen, renewed by Ellery Queen, reprinted by permission of the Estate of Ellery Queen. **Damon Runyon:** "Butch Minds the Baby" from *Favorites* by Damon Runyon, copyright 1930 by P. F. Collier and Son, Inc.; copyright renewed © 1957 by Damon Runyon, Jr. and Mary Runyon McCann. Reprinted by special arrangement with American Play Company, Inc., Sheldon Abend, Pres., 19 West 44th Street, Suite 1204, New York, N.Y. 10036. **Dorothy L. Sayers:** "The Inspiration of Mr. Budd" from *In the Teeth of Evidence and Other Mysteries* by Dorothy L. Sayers (Hodder & Stoughton Ltd) reprinted by permission of David Higham Associates Ltd. **Raymond Smullyan:** Puzzles and solutions nos. 71, 72, 73, 77, 78, 79, 80 from *What is the Name of This Book?—The Riddle of Dracula & Other Logical Puzzles* by Raymond Smullyan (Prentice-Hall, 1978) reprinted by permission of the author. **Michael Underwood:** "Murder at St. Oswald's" from *Verdict on Thirteen: A Detective Club Anthology* by Michael Underwood (Faber, 1979) reprinted by permission of A. M. Heath & Co. Ltd. on behalf of the author. **Andrew Vachss:** "It's a Hard World" from *Born Bad* by Andrew Vachss, copyright © 1994 by Andrew Vachss, reprinted by permission of Vintage Books, a division of Random House, Inc.

Every effort has been made to obtain permission to reproduce copyright material but there may be cases where we have been unable to contact a copyright holder The publisher will be happy to correct any omissions in future printings.

Titles in the Story Library Series